HISTORY & BEYOND

Edited by Jenni Bannister

Years of  Young**Writers**

First published in Great Britain in 2016 by:

Young**Writers**

Remus House
Coltsfoot Drive
Peterborough
PE2 9BF
Telephone: 01733 890066
Website: www.youngwriters.co.uk

FOREWORD

Welcome, Reader!

For Young Writers' latest competition we gave school children nationwide the task of writing a story about time travel, either past or future. Alternatively they could write on any subject of their choice. The challenge was to create a beginning, middle and an end in just 100 words, and they rose to it magnificently!

We chose stories for publication based on style, expression and imagination. The result is this entertaining collection full of diverse and imaginative mini sagas, which is also a delightful keepsake to look back on in years to come.

Here at Young Writers our aim is to encourage creativity in children and to inspire a love of the written word, so it's great to get such an amazing response, with some absolutely fantastic stories. This made it a tough challenge to pick the winners, so well done to Alex Mintram-Chattell who has been chosen as the best author in this anthology.

I'd like to congratulate all the young authors in Time-Travelling Tales - History & Beyond - I hope this inspires them to continue with their creative writing. And who knows, maybe we'll be seeing their names on the best seller lists in the future...

Jenni Bannister

Editorial Manager

CONTENTS

Eton Park Junior School, Burton-On-Trent

Grangewood Independent School, London

Halstead Community Primary School, Sevenoaks

Hospital Education Service, Coventry

Laindon Park Primary School, Basildon

The Viking School, Skegness

THE
MINI SAGAS

The Big Bang

Confusion fizzed up inside of Josh. He noticed his watch was ticking faster than normal. Seconds later, he felt nauseous and collapsed. Suddenly, he awoke to a stagnant smell in an overcrowded tavern. A slender man sporting a cropped beard bumped into Josh, spilling mead over him. 'Mine fault, youngst'r,' acknowledged the stranger, 'cometh joineth me.'

'Sure… ' stammered Josh.

'Leteth him be!' came a gruff voice, resonating from a group of men huddled intently around a table.

The stranger smiled at Josh, 'Mine nameth be Guido Fawkes, mine friends calleth me Guy.'

'I need to stop them,' gasped Josh.

Laila Atif (11)

Time Travel Adventure

The world as we know it has been destroyed. WW3 has taken place and there is nothing left. I have to go back and do my best to prevent it. I have to use my time machine to make sure that this war is over before it has a chance to begin, before the cancer has time to spread. You will never thank me, I will never be famous. If I succeed no one will ever know my name because all of this will never have happened. But I will know that I saved the world.

Liam Heron (11)

Time Travelling Tales

One afternoon, the minibus was taking me home from school and was hit by lightning. The blast made the bus travel at the speed of light. When the bus stopped I couldn't believe my eyes... dinosaurs! We were back in time.
We took the emergency axe. Roars were everywhere. A T-rex appeared. We ran. The bus driver was too slow and was eaten. The axe flew up and I caught it. I threw it at the T-rex and he fell. I picked up the bloody axe. There were more dinosaurs to kill. This was not the end... just the beginning!

Mark Heron (9)

Time Travelling Adventure

A hole in the ground, a silver ball... a spaceship! I entered.
Lady with pink hair. Picked to time travel to year 3,000. In the blink of an eye, she disappeared. Everything went black, a voice said, 'Travelling to the year 3,000... you've arrived.' A hologram appeared, I was the chosen one. Armour and a weapon. My quest: to find the vandals, stop them destroying the future. Others had failed.
I knew what to do. Enter the vandals' hideout, have strength to defeat them. Hold my sword up. An epic battle, I was victorious.
Back to the spaceship, return home.

Emma Heron (8)

Time Travelling To Downing Street

I was going to my grandad's attic to get some games to play. I saw boxes and I went closer to them. One had many levers and numbers. I typed in my grandad's birthday, 19 December 1943. A swivel of dust swerved around me and when my eyes opened I saw a man in a suit smoking a cigar. I also saw a black door and the number ten. Then I realised I was in front of 10 Downing Street. I saw the machine which took me there. I put it back to 2015 and arrived back at the attic.

Jasraj Hans (10)
Beehive Preparatory School, Ilford

Dazed And Amazed Future

I fell out of a portal, dazed, crazed and amazed. I did it! I went to the future! I picked myself off the... purple grass? I glanced around and saw I was at a robotic park. I heard bleeping behind me. I saw R2D2, well a descendant. He said, 'Welcome stranger to the year 2222. Hey wanna explore this never-ending city?'
'OK,' I said, following him. I saw humans weirdly dressed like they were half-robot. Then a piercing scream broke the day. 'Go back home!' he yelled tapping my time belt, teleporting me home again, dazed and amazed.

Nafeesa Khan
Beehive Preparatory School, Ilford

The Park

Me and my mum and dad were having a walk. We saw some trees which we had never seen before. We'd come to this park before and had not seen it. We went closer and we saw a tree house. Dad said, 'Let's go in it.'
Me and Mum were scared. We followed Dad up the ladder. We heard a noise, it said, 'Who's there?'
We got back down and ran deeper into the forest. We got ourselves lost. I was worried. What would happen to us? We found a path and ran back home.

Sofiyya Azam (8)
Beehive Preparatory School, Ilford

Stary's Mission

One day, there was a boy called Stary, he was eleven-years-old. He lived in a village with his mum and dad. Suddenly, I came to the year that Stary was in. It looked so different to me. Me and Stary were friends so we decided to go to a park. When we got back his parents were gone! So me and Stary had to go on a mission to find Stary's parents. We went in a vortex to find his parents. Me and Stary found his mum and dad. Then Stary went home and they relaxed.

Zaydan Hussain (7)
Beehive Preparatory School, Ilford

4

A Visit To The Future

'Finally!' I whispered. I had snuck into a science lab. As I entered the lab I saw a time machine. I just really wanted a trip to the future. So I hopped into it and it flew into the sky. It flew around the world. Now I was in the future.

Everything that used to have wheels now had rectangular shapes that allowed them to hover.

One of the buttons blew up. The time machine didn't work. I noticed that everyone nowadays had time machines.

I found another time machine and went back to the present. 'I'm back!' I shouted.

Arjun Rastogi (9)
Beehive Preparatory School, Ilford

Time Machine

I got the metal and plastic. I started building my masterpiece machine. Finally, I finished it! I finished my time machine. I stumbled in my time machine and I set the time to 2013 and in three seconds, *bang!* The time machine was in the sky and suddenly fell onto the ground.

I opened the door. Wow! I was amazed it worked. I went to the future, I saw flying cars. I was amazed. I went back to 1901. I told all my friends about it. My adventure was very, very fun. My friends said, 'Let's go next!'

Ibraheem Ali (8)
Beehive Preparatory School, Ilford

Untitled

Once upon a time, in the Victorian times, there was a very poor family who had no money.

One Christmas, the dad went to work. As he was walking he was feeling depressed as he felt he could not give his family a good Christmas. He then tripped over some leaves and found some money on the floor next to him. He got so excited, he picked up the money and ran to the toy shop to buy his children everything they'd ever dreamed of having. That Christmas, when the children opened their presents, they were the happiest children alive.

Alisha Patel (7)
Beehive Preparatory School, Ilford

The Time Machine

I found a box, an unusual-looking box. I tried to find Mum's pearls but they were nowhere to be found, so I went inside the box. Suddenly, it jolted back in time. Once I arrived, I found a colossal dinosaur! I tried to find them but they were nowhere to be found. When I went inside the box, it fell to the ground and I ended up in the year 3055. I found Mum's pearls floating in the air. I quickly went back inside the box and it finally took me home, when I could give Mum's pearls back.

Wahy Yahya (10)
Beehive Preparatory School, Ilford

The Time Hand

Ben was on a school trip, he was lost. He found a hand and put it on. He ran screaming, 'Get it off, it's stuck!' He ran to his friend. Burno tried using a chainsaw, it didn't work. He saw a button and pressed it and Ben time-travelled to a volcano, and the hand was out of battery. It needed to warm up. It was ready to time travel again. This time he travelled to the dinosaurs and they were hunting for him. He saw a dark cave. He hid in it then saw a comet coming at him...

Feroz Malik
Beehive Preparatory School, Ilford

Back To The Titanic

'What's this?' There was this large machine by the sofa. I sat in the seat. *Bang!* I closed my eyes. When I opened them, I was in this strange place.
'Welcome to the Titanic,' boomed a voice from the top deck. I ran to the bridge. I was about to tell the captain how I got there when the ship jolted. It hit an iceberg.
'Get off the ship!' I bellowed. They didn't listen. I ran back to the time machine. It was too late. The machine had bounded into the water. How was I going to get back home?

Lamiyah Shafique Adam (10)
Beehive Preparatory School, Ilford

Meeting Galileo

Whizz, chucka-choo-choo! The time machine spun to the word 'past'. Its metallic arms grabbed hold of me. *Thump!* I was in the Stuart period, 1609-1610. I saw a bright gleaming light in front of me, but quite a way up. I knew who it was. It was Galileo. I sprinted through the door and Galileo came running downstairs. He greeted me and told me to come upstairs. He showed me how he'd constructed the telescope. I gave Galileo some recommendation. When *whizz, chucka-choo,* came. I jumped into my time machine. *Boom! Bang! Whizz! Chucka-choo! Pop!* I'd reached home.

Jeevakan Annanthakumar (10)
Beehive Preparatory School, Ilford

Back To World War II

He hauled the tarpaulin off. The machine was covered with buttons and levers. We sat down. Dad forced a lever forward. We were gone! I opened my eyes and I was in a field with my dad a couple of metres away from me. Immediately a squadron of planes flew over us but didn't see us. Grandad had told us where he lived during World War II. It had to be there. We raced through London. We crept into Grandad's house and found the machine. Dad poked a button and we were back. 'Argh!' *Fizz, whallop, bang!* I was gone.

Ibrahim Azam (10)
Beehive Preparatory School, Ilford

Astonishing Aliens

Through a portal, Stephen Stone found himself in the year 2500. 'Where are the humans? They're extinct now, aliens ruled the Earth!' he shouted. As he walked in this time period he discovered aliens were intelligent creatures and could transform into anything, first a jaguar then a tiger. Suddenly, the aliens saw him, chased him and when they got hold of him they put him behind an electrical prison where the other time-travellers were kept for being human and coming to this mysterious time period.

After years, Stephen escaped. He is still out there somewhere trying to get home...

Kian Patel (11)
Beehive Preparatory School, Ilford

Back To Hastings

One day, Mike and his friend Joe found a portal in Japan. Mike and Joe decided to go into it. Mike and Joe were in Normandy in the Middle Ages. They were involved in the Battle of Hastings. Mike and Joe rowed the raft to Hastings. Mike and Joe had heavy armour, colossal swords and mammoth shields to protect them in battle. Mike and Joe had a few injuries. Mike saw somebody who killed King Harold. The person who killed Harold became the invisible king. A particular baron didn't like the king because he'd killed the other king of England...

Hassan Ahmed (8)
Beehive Preparatory School, Ilford

The Dinosaurs

Frank was playing football with his friends. The bully, Steve, tackled him. Frank fell in the invisible time machine. It went whirring and turning. As soon as the boy fell out, he was placed in a jungle which was freezing cold. The boy saw many trees and volcanoes. He saw large dinosaurs. The dinosaurs roared. They munched the leaves and saw the little boy. They went close to the boy. The small boy threw the leaves at the dinosaurs. Then they became friends. The boy taught them English and the he never left them behind. He lived happily ever after.

Maathavan Annanthakumar (8)
Beehive Preparatory School, Ilford

My Dad And Me

My dad got the foil and stuffed it down the hole. Suddenly, I woke up, I went downstairs. I said to my dad, 'Dad I've just had an idea on how to make a time machine.'
He replied, 'I doubt if it'll work.'
'But it's worth a go.'
We used my dad's car. We made a hole at the top for foil. We got the plastic and metal. My dad got the foil and stuffed it down the hole. We were ready. I got in the car and set the time. We got out of the car. But my dad…

Amrith Singaravelou (8)
Beehive Preparatory School, Ilford

Our Roman Adventure!

My brother and I went in a time machine to the Romans in 43 AD. We walked around the town. Whilst walking, we saw gladiators heading to the Coliseum. We sat down on a chair and saw the Romans fight. The Romans were competing against other Romans. They saw us. When the battle finished, the Romans who were fighting against each other wanted me to be with them. If I didn't they were going to kill me. My brother got a sword, shield and defeated them.

Tasneem Delawala (8)
Beehive Preparatory School, Ilford

The Time Machine

The wind was blowing and the sky was dark. Two boys were telling jokes and went into the technology lab, and went into the time machine. *Poof!* They were in the time 2021. Tazrian and Ramyan could tell that because there was a huge sign that said '2021'. They were happy the time machine worked. It was only the first time they'd tried their masterpiece but there was one problem, they needed a piece of the world's largest battery but they didn't know where it was. They were struggling but they were getting used to the future.

Tazrian Mamun (7)
Beehive Preparatory School, Ilford

A Wild Animal Hunt

It was a mysterious, chilly night in the rainforest. Two explorers were searching for wild animals. They managed to capture a picture of a vicious lion and a fierce tiger. The curious explorers snapped a picture of the wild animals which came out hideous. 'We cannot show this to other explorers!' they exclaimed. Suddenly, they were transported back in time. They then went on to search for more wild animals with pleasing faces. The explorers trekked a long, long time until finally they came face-to-face with an animal whose face was as pleasant as the moon.

Zenab Ghori (8)
Beehive Preparatory School, Ilford

Clash Of The Cats

In 1996 there was a kitten called Olive. She seemed nice but really she was terrifying. Her dream was to take over the world. She decided to put her plan into action. She got all the cats she knew and gathered them. Olive told them her plan and they all set out to do it. They went all around Britain. The humans said, 'Go!' but the cats stayed for longer than expected.
Nineteen years went past. The cats stayed. In 2015, the humans surrendered and cats took over Britain. Who knows what will happen? Cats are cleverer than we think…

Anika Maher
Bishop Winnington-Ingram CE Primary School, Ruislip

Jungle World

Once upon a time Jessica decided to go on holiday to Scotland. She bought the ticket a few weeks before her trip online. The day she had to travel, she went to work with her luggage so that she could get her train from work, as the train station was close to her office. By 4pm she boarded the train to Scotland. On her way, she dozed off and woke a couple of hours later. She was in the Safari with the animals. She enjoyed herself at the Safari and she made friends with animals but she had to go.

Janet Mbonu (8)
Bishop Winnington-Ingram CE Primary School, Ruislip

Lilly And Tallulah's Fairy Friends Save The Day

Lilly and Tallulah are two best friends that are secretly friends with magical fairies. They go on a school trip to a museum for a sleepover with their class. They stop at a service station for a break and while out of their coach, Lilly and Tallulah spot goblins trying to steal their overnight bags. Their friends, the magical fairies came to help them. The water fairy soaks the goblins so they drop the bags and run away. The fairies put the bags back onto the coach before anybody spots them. The girls' fairy friends have saved the day again.

Brooke Bo Povey (7)
Bishop Winnington-Ingram CE Primary School, Ruislip

Snowstorm

One day I woke up and my mum told me that it was about to start snowing. So I was very happy. We had breakfast and put our shoes and coats on and packed our bags. Then we got in the car and set off. But there was a snowstorm and we were stuck in it for half an hour. Then everyone who lived nearby got out their shovels and scooped the snow out of the way. But when we got to school it was closed, so we had to go through all the traffic all over again.

Dhanvi Morzaria (7)
Bishop Winnington-Ingram CE Primary School, Ruislip

The Dinosaurs

Millions of years ago, dinosaurs ruled the planet Earth. My story is about a dinosaur called Elliot and he is a triceratops.
One sunny morning, Elliot went out for a walk. After a while, Elliot was starving. Elliot found some crunchy, juicy, yummy, delicious, scrumptiously succulent branches on the tall, nearby tree. Suddenly, a T-rex came out of nowhere. The T-rex tried to attack Elliot, but Elliot pushed with his horns. All of a sudden, the ground shook and a nearby hill exploded with boiling-hot, steaming lava. T-rex ran and Elliot was safe.

Max Savov (7)
Bishop Winnington-Ingram CE Primary School, Ruislip

Spike The Hero

Peter and his dog Spike went to the forest for a picnic. Peter and Spike loved playing together. When they were in the forest, Peter was throwing a ball for Spike. Suddenly, Peter tripped over a big stone and he fell down. He couldn't move. When Spike saw that, he ran for help to Peter's parents. The parents followed Spike and found Peter lying on the grass. They took him to hospital because his leg was broken. Spike acted like a hero. After, they all went home. For Spike's bravery, the parents bought him a big bone.

Maciej Borkowski (7)
Bishop Winnington-Ingram CE Primary School, Ruislip

The Police Saved Jamie's Birthday

It was Jamie's birthday, he was extremely happy. He went downstairs and realised his presents were gone. Suddenly, his mum and dad realised what happened.
They all got frustrated, felt weird and said, 'I'm sure we bought presents!'
Then they decided they should call the police, so they did! The police turned up and tried to investigate this mystery. Finally, after a very long time, they solved the crime and told them it was a monster. The police captured the mighty monster and put him in jail.
'Phew, I got to enjoy my birthday!' declared Jamie, scoffing his birthday cake.

Jack Philip Baker (7)
Bishop Winnington-Ingram CE Primary School, Ruislip

Kirsty's Magical Adventure

Once there was a girl called Kirsty and she had a horse called Ginger. One day a letter came and it said that Kirsty was allowed to enter a competition. She was very happy about this and decided to do lots of practise. Days went by and Kirsty got excited. Finally, the day arrived. The race began and halfway through she twisted her shoulder, so she went home very upset. But she made a wish. The wish came true! Kirsty got back onto Ginger's back and started racing again. Finally, Kirsty won the race and got a trophy and medal.

Daisy Smith-Keating (7)
Bishop Winnington-Ingram CE Primary School, Ruislip

Cindey's Great Adventure

In a little village lived a poor family in China and the only thing that they could live on was sticky rice. So one hot day Cindey was fed up with living on rice every day, so she told her Grandma Ni that she was fed up. Grandma Ni said, 'I've got a story for you.' Then Cindey started to realise that not many people had food. So she set off the next day to Korea. She saw so many poor people like her and she learned to never complain and to be grateful for everything she already had.

Moriah E Ikuthyinu (11)
Bishop Winnington-Ingram CE Primary School, Ruislip

16

Now You See Me, Now You Don't. I'm In WWII!

'Mum, where is my cap? Now I am going to be late for school!'
'Hey Jim!'
'Hey Tom, like your outfit!'
'Yours too.' Tom turned off his phone and went in the classroom with his evacuee outfit on.
'You boy, over here now. Where is your suitcase? We have to get to the station, the evacuation train leaves at ten.'
Tom was bewildered, this was weird. Where was his teacher? Where were his friends? Suddenly, a siren sounded. 'Get down under the tables!' *Boom!* Silence. Then laughing. 'Everybody out now!' Tom left the classroom. Playground, modern uniform, back to 2015.

Isabella Rebecca Burchell (10)
Bishop Winnington-Ingram CE Primary School, Ruislip

Land Of The Dinosaurs!

There once was a girl called Lucy. For years she'd been working on a contraption to pursue her dreams of meeting the dinosaurs. Today was the day; in just a second Lucy would flick the lever of the time travel machine (as she called it) and go where no one had gone before. Three, two, one... *Poof!* It had worked! Whilst wandering around, Lucy encountered many dinosaurs and new things we would never have thought existed, like trees that sparkled and fish on land! However, it was getting late, she had to go. But where had the machine gone... ?

Lucy Wilcock
Bishop Winnington-Ingram CE Primary School, Ruislip

The Bad Sharpener

'Huh? I'm alive, I'm alive!' shouted the big pencil.
'Not for long!' exclaimed the sharpener. So he sharpened the pencil to make him three times smaller. Then the pencil cried, 'Why, why do you do this to me?'
He cried, 'Because it's funny!'
After that, the bad sharpener did that every day until one day he sharpened him so much he was a tiny pencil!
'Please stop!' said the little pencil.
'Once more...' *Pop!* The pencil disappeared into thin air! 'Oh no, what have I done?' He was so small he'd disappeared. So the evil bad sharpener never came back.

Yousif Fahmi (10)
Bishop Winnington-Ingram CE Primary School, Ruislip

Super Bob And The Attacked City

One quiet afternoon in the city the shops were busy and full.
The next day Bob heard everybody screaming because there was a super villain called Super Bee. He wanted to attack the city. But who could stop him? Bob could! So he didn't go to bed overnight, he transformed into a superhero – was the whole city attacked by then? Quickly, he ran to the city and smacked, kicked and stomped Super Bee down to the floor. Everyone cheered at Super Bob because he saved the city from Super Bee. The city was all peaceful after the attack.

Angel Fawcett (8)
Bishop Winnington-Ingram CE Primary School, Ruislip

18

The Wood Animal Friends

One frosty morning the woodland animals met at the frozen duck pond. They were going skating. Mrs Rabbit was expecting so she was at home in her burrow asleep. She had told no one about this. Miss Duck realised that Mrs Rabbit wasn't there. She stopped on the ice, letting everyone fall over her.

'What was that for?' exclaimed the animals.

'Mrs Rabbit is missing!'

They set off through the snow to Mrs Rabbit's house and knocked on the door. Mrs Rabbit answered and told them her news. They were so excited they started knitting straight away like old women.

Charlotte Axten (8)
Bishop Winnington-Ingram CE Primary School, Ruislip

The Mystery Of The Mythical Animals

Once upon a time there was a boy called Tom. One day he saw a magic portal in his house and went inside it. After that, he was in a weird place with mythical animals. Suddenly, the mythical animals attacked Tom but Tom escaped and found a little house with a goblin. Tom asked, 'Can you help me?'

The goblin replied, 'How can I help you?'

'The mythical animals are attacking me,' Tom said.

'OK, you're lucky that I created a potion for that. Do you want to go back home or calm the animals?'

'Home!' So he left.

Iago Regueira (8)
Bishop Winnington-Ingram CE Primary School, Ruislip

Tommy's Christmas

It was Christmas time at Tommy's house.
One day he was arguing with his mum because she wouldn't let him play in the snow. Tommy was rude to his mum. She sent him to bed early that night. Santa came to visit Tommy and told him that his mum loved him very much.
Tommy woke up the next day and went into his mum for a huge cuddle. He said he was sorry. They spent the day cooking Christmas cookies and decorated the tree. Tommy's mum was very happy Tommy was being good. Just in time for Christmas Day.

Harry Swinton (8)
Bishop Winnington-Ingram CE Primary School, Ruislip

The Magic Whistle

Real Madrid and Yeovil football teams line up ready to kick off. The referee takes his whistle out of his pocket. He blows his whistle and the ball disappears. The ball is invisible, how can the game go on? The players keep on playing but Real Madrid keeps scoring all of the goals. The referee does not understand what has happened to his whistle. Sneaky Ronaldo had swapped the whistle for a magic whistle. The referee gave Ronaldo a red card and sent him off the pitch, but Real Madrid had already won 5,000 to nil.

Lewis Dargue (7)
Bishop Winnington-Ingram CE Primary School, Ruislip

The Elf Who Saved Christmas

Eathen Elf stared in horror as the evil reindeer swiped the presents for the naughty children. Grabbing Rudolph, Eathen raced to retrieve them. Moments later, the courageous pair entered a savage snowstorm. A white blanket of snow covered their entire bodies.
'Please help us!' shouted Eathen, gripping onto Rudolph.
In the distance appeared a tall young boy with ice-blue eyes. With all his might, Frost blew the snow from the icy cold pair and it flew like a bird covering all the evil reindeer. Eathen grabbed the presents and brought them back to the workshop for the good children.

Millie Emma Baker (7)
Bishop Winnington-Ingram CE Primary School, Ruislip

Ella Went Hunting

One day Ella was hunting for animals in the jungle. Ella was following the trail on her map when she heard the sound of an elephant. So Ella left the trail to look for the elephant but she couldn't find it. Ella got lost!
At Ella's home her mum and dad were worried because she hadn't come back for dinner. So they organised a search party. They searched the jungle and yelled, 'Ella!'
Ella heard them and shouted back. They heard her shouting and went to her. Everyone was happy that they had found her. Ella was very happy.

Tabitha Rose Goffey (7)
Bishop Winnington-Ingram CE Primary School, Ruislip

It's Not Nice To Be Alone

Once upon a time there was a naughty boy who always got in trouble at school. Once he said something bad to a child from school. Another time he splashed water on a child's head. In the class he was making noise. All the time he was punished by the teacher.

He didn't want to change so he ended up alone, with no friends. He didn't like to be alone so he asked his mum to help him. His mum told him to be nice and friendly. He started to change and behave nicely. He started to make friends again.

Rares Pancs (8)
Bishop Winnington-Ingram CE Primary School, Ruislip

A Dreaming Princess!

One frosty and still evening a beautiful princess named Laura tucked into her warm royal bed. That night, her dream took her on an adventure she could never forget!

All of a sudden, her favourite Barbie doll was cooking delicious sugary doughnuts for Daisy the puppy and Squashy the rabbit. The fast toy cars were having a race and Tom the cat was painting a wintry picture for Laura.

Laura realised that her toys had come alive! She jumped out of bed to join in but her toys couldn't see her. The race cars *swooshed* past and she woke up!

Victoria Strelnikova (7)
Bishop Winnington-Ingram CE Primary School, Ruislip

Journey For A Robot

'Help!' said Elisha.
'Hey!' they both replied.
'What's wrong?'
'We're moving!'
'Wh... '
Crash!
'What was that?' asked Jayden.
'Let's check it out!'
'What's this?' asked Elisha.
James picked it up.
'Wow! That just moved!' said Jayden.
It spoke in a robotic voice, 'Follow me.'
They must've travelled 100 miles before it finally said, 'We're here!'
'What is it?' asked James
'My ship.' it replied. It told them to start digging...
'Hey! I found something!' exclaimed Jayden
Finally, they dug all of it up.
'Whoah! It's amazing!' shouted Elisha.
In the morning they said their last goodbyes, or did they...?

James Wright (11)
Bishop Winnington-Ingram CE Primary School, Ruislip

Emily's Adventure

'Oh what a lovely place,' said Emily to her Dad. He was waiting for her hot dog. Then a flash made her fall over. When she woke up Henry VIII was there and cried, 'Who are you?'
Emily whispered, 'Emily, oh and I can also make a burger.' So she made a burger for Henry VIII. Then the flash whisked her back to Winter Wonderland. 'Argh!' shouted Emily. Then she woke up and said, 'Oh Dad you don't know how glad I am to see you!'
'OK,' said Dad.
Then Emily bit into her hot dog. 'Yum yum yippee!'

Lilly Charlotte Everett (7)
Bishop Winnington-Ingram CE Primary School, Ruislip

History Writer

Did you know that sorcerers live in mankind's midst? Hitler died unexpectedly because of levitating bullets, whilst the terrible truth behind Queen Victoria is that the black she always wore was actually typical sorcerers' uniform. In fact, between you and me, I am one too... I teleported back to Hitler's reign over fear and hatred. He saw me and screamed something German I would rather *not* translate. Then he held me by the collar and tried to stab me. I used levitating bullets in self-defence. The next thing I saw was a picture of Churchill – my job was done!

Caleb Huang (10)
Bishop Winnington-Ingram CE Primary School, Ruislip

A New Life In The Unknown!

One summer's day a family of five were all on their Apple iPhones until the oldest saw a picture of a bonfire and wanted one so bad that her mum whispered, 'OK.'
Later on, whilst it was happening, her parents were fighting. So the youngest decided to wander off. Until she saw a pitch-black mouldy cave in the corner of her eye, then disappeared. She came out scared and saw a tall castle and went in. The lady knew her and gave her a chip to get home. When she got there it didn't look like her home...

Elliemay Huggar (10)
Bishop Winnington-Ingram CE Primary School, Ruislip

The Magical Mystery

The royal school opened its door to Danielle the princess. She didn't fit in well with the others. Everyone took the mick out of her, saying she didn't deserve to be there because she didn't grow up in a fancy palace like the others.
Instead she lived in a normal house in Swindon. There was a girl at school named Charlie, she took it too far and became Danielle's worst enemy.
But one day an unexpected visitor came to the school and surprised everyone with some news.
'Danielle and Charlie are sisters. Take a look, you're real sisters!'
'Are we?'

Nicole Williams (10)
Bishop Winnington-Ingram CE Primary School, Ruislip

Pure Insanity

Dario first saw it lying there untouched and unnoticed. It was as if he was meant to read it. Golden block letters imprinted the hardback mystery: 'Pure Insanity'. As Dario gently tapped his fingers across it, his world changed. Blue sky was now neon green as madness arrived for his next victim. Orange beings skipped through the... wait... *alive trees!* As if the world was completely normal. All of a sudden, darkness came through the light; love became hate and evil overcame but then the book appeared. Dario ran to it and then all was well. This is pure insanity!

Adon Tomas
Bishop Winnington-Ingram CE Primary School, Ruislip

Time Travel To The Great Fire Of London

Ding! Ding! Ding! The school bell screamed into the children of BWI school's ears. School had ended. Toby jumped on the school bus, which he did every day, hoping to have a safe journey home. Well that certainly didn't happen... *Cough! Cough! Cough!* There was smoke everywhere you glanced, it was chaos! Toby sprinted out the red bus' door. He smelt smoke, he saw fire.
'Run!' shouted the man. *Stumble, trip, stumble, trip.* The people ran as fast as lightning and hopped on a boat. Toby had learnt this in BWI Primary School, it was the Great Fire of London.

Jayden Evans (10)
Bishop Winnington-Ingram CE Primary School, Ruislip

26

That One Rose...

One summer day a farmer planted a red rose in a meadow under an oak tree. It grew extremely fast and inherited an odour that was enough to suffocate you. It was late in the day when a twelve-year-old girl named Lily found the rose. She sat down by the rose and dreamed and soon it hit midnight. The moon shone down onto the rose and then Lily inhaled the rose's scent and suddenly the rose started wilting, while Lily started fading away. The farmer saw what was happening so he picked the rose but Lily was gone...

Katie Patricia Hall (11)
Bishop Winnington-Ingram CE Primary School, Ruislip

Tragedy At The Airport

One ordinary day at an ordinary airport a man called Tom was going to Barbados and on his way there was tragedy. In security he walked through and then, *Beep! Beep! Beep!* The guards rushed towards him, checked him and then suddenly they pulled out a tarantula. They argued about it and then they called the police. Then he went to court, then off to prison. He spent three days in there until *boom!* The walls collapsed and he was free! Out of the gloom his friend came running to him, he was saved! Then off to home he went!

Dominic Stevens (10)
Bishop Winnington-Ingram CE Primary School, Ruislip

Survival

Suffocating. That's all I can remember until now. I woke hungry, thirsty but most of all, puzzled. I tried to walk but my body was shaking.
'Rooarr!'
My body moved suddenly. 'Argh!' I knew it was coming towards me.
'Argh!' It was in front of me, I couldn't walk, my whole body was dead but my soul was still alive. I kept running but then the beast stopped and spoke. I couldn't believe what I was hearing. Was it true? However my mind couldn't take it and I fainted. As I woke, I realised that it was all a dream.

Reneé Renner-Thomas
Bishop Winnington-Ingram CE Primary School, Ruislip

The Sinking Boat

It was a nice and lovely day, so my parents had decided that we could go on a boat ride on the sea. Everyone agreed so we all sat in the car and had already set off.
It was twenty minutes later that we had arrived. Everyone got out of the car and started to walk nearer to the boat. Eventually, we had got in the boat and drifted off. Suddenly, the boat hit an iceberg! Luckily, in the distance we had seen another boat so everyone swam to it. We finally told Albert to drop us home.

Kulraj Juttla
Bishop Winnington-Ingram CE Primary School, Ruislip

Warning From The Future

You may think time travelling is not possible, but I know different. I've been there to the future. I mean it's not like you would imagine it. The Earth does not exist like we know it. It's been destroyed by the way that humans have lived. We cut down the rainforests affecting the animals and the climate. We didn't stop burning fossil fuels so global warming meant the polar caps melted and caused flooding. Have I actually been to the future? No I haven't. It isn't possible. But what I've described is possible if we don't change our ways. Help!

Joseph Robertson
Bishop Winnington-Ingram CE Primary School, Ruislip

Mermaid Land

Once in a far land there was a girl called Scarlet and she was on holiday with her parents. She was in Spain. She liked it there but when Scarlet saw the swimming pool she was really thrilled because she couldn't wait to go. So she got dressed in her summer dress and then they crossed the busy road to get the train and they got to go swimming. She accidentally went into the deep pool and when she went down she saw a beautiful mermaid. She took Scarlet to Mermaid Land. Then Scarlet went back home.

Marisa Yorke (7)
Bishop Winnington-Ingram CE Primary School, Ruislip

An Unexpected World...!

It all started on a groovy morning. When a young boy named Timothy was playing in his garden. While he was in his mysterious garden, he spotted a hole in the ground. He went right up to the hole and thought it would be funny to jump into the hole. The hole was a dark, horrible, smelly place and it took a long time to reach the bottom. When he finally got to the bottom, a half-monkey, half-donkey grabbed his hand and took him back to California. Before they reached California, Dingango said, 'Don't come here again.'

Louise Williams-Ralph (10)
Bishop Winnington-Ingram CE Primary School, Ruislip

88mph

A man called Arno Dorian found a car but it was not an ordinary car, it was a time machine. He hopped inside and started the engine. He turned around to see on the back seats something in the shape of a Y and it had a note taped to it reading, 'Do not start the engine and especially do not go 88mph. EB.'
His mind was a tornado of questions. *Why not go 88mph? Who is EB? What does EB stand for?* Well Arno had already started the engine, he might as well go 88mph.

Luke Timewell (11)
Bishop Winnington-Ingram CE Primary School, Ruislip

The Queen And The Maze

Once upon a time there was a queen and king fairy. The queen was very bored so she went outside into the royal maze but got lost. She made a flare with her magic but the maze was too tall. The king couldn't find the queen and was very worried. He asked the cook where the queen might be?

The cook said, 'She went to the maze.'

The king went to rescue her. She shouted, 'Yay!' When the king found her. There was a joyful feast in honour of her return.

Meghan Elizabeth Campion (8)
Bishop Winnington-Ingram CE Primary School, Ruislip

The Christmas Day When I Lost My Presents

Once upon a time my family woke up on Christmas Day. We looked at the presents and wanted a drink so we went downstairs and got a drink. We went back upstairs and the presents had disappeared. We found the monster taking more so we followed him to his cave and went in. We took the presents back home and enjoyed the rest of Christmas Day as a family.

Sienna May Hanna (7)
Bishop Winnington-Ingram CE Primary School, Ruislip

The Future Car

James was near a restaurant when he saw a truck which made a noise. The truck's back opened up and out came a future car. James' father was in the future car with Bobby the dog. James climbed into the car. James' father accidentally pressed the wrong code on the car computer. They went to Australia where his grandparents lived. The car took them to the 1890s. His grandparents were still babies. They fixed the computer but it took a long time to rebuild the engine. Then they flew home back to the garage. Then James took the taxi home.

Noah Sanders (8)
Bishop Winnington-Ingram CE Primary School, Ruislip

Bear Cub Finds A Family

Crying could be heard in the forest. Bear Cub was sad because he didn't have a family. All of a sudden there was a noise and a boy and a girl appeared in the sunlight on the forest path. The bear cub and the boy and girl saw each other and although at first they were all scared, they soon began to notice that the bear cub was lost and needed to be loved. So the boy and the girl took the bear cub home. Where there was originally tears, the bear cub now had love, laughter and cuddles.

Chiara Lawford (7)
Bishop Winnington-Ingram CE Primary School, Ruislip

The Adventure Of Grandma Joe!

During the days when I was young I had found a ruby-red cloak covering a large object. With curiosity, I slowly walked towards it. I pulled the cloak off to reveal a bracelet with an image of a scorpion. I got sucked into it!

When I opened my eyes, my mouth fell open in astonishment. I saw chocolate flowers, however I won't tell you how good they tasted because it would only make your mouth water in vain! I heard a harsh voice! I froze in terror and this, my children, is why this is on my back...

Jasmin Ahmadzai
Colindale Primary School, London

The Unknown World

I found a gold, heart-shaped necklace on the floor. It was so pretty it had to be worn so I put it on. *Whoosh!* I zoomed up into the air and spun around lots of times until I was dizzy. I landed in the middle of a bridge over a lake. All that was in view was Big Ben standing in the distance. There was no one around, I was definitely alone. I raced to Big Ben and noticed that the clock wasn't moving. 'Hello, is anyone here?' Something tapped me on the shoulder, I thought I was alone...

Safia Irfan (8)
Colindale Primary School, London

Under The Sea

I walked into my room which was decorated like the ocean, when suddenly the wallpaper came to life! Fish, mermaids and seashells started peeling off my wall. Consequently, I felt wet when I realised that I was under the sea!

I sat down on a rock to ponder, when a terrifying sea monster captured me! It was the most petrifying time of my life! I kept shouting for my mum whilst she was fast asleep! Instead a mermaid named Ariel saved me and gave me a beautiful seashell bracelet that changed me into a mermaid.

Riona Byqmeti
Colindale Primary School, London

The Magical Toy Chest

I decided to rummage through my toy chest, there had to be something good in here. I paused and stared gloomily at the toy in my hand, which I didn't recognise. I thought off the top of my head it might be a miniature time machine! 'That's ridiculous!' Michel muttered gregariously.

'No look, it must be.' I anxiously pressed on the buttons of a tiny keyboard typing the year 3456, nervously waiting to see what happened. I could not believe my eyes; I saw hoverboards. People were flying, there was even magic! I was definitely not expecting this...

Sophie Azari
Colindale Primary School, London

The Time Travelling Adventure

I tripped over and saw black! Where was I? Suddenly, I opened my eyes and saw robots everywhere. Was I in the future? No that isn't possible, or is it? Then a robot shouted in his deep voice, 'What species are you?'

'I'm a human,' I cried timidly. ' A human is a living thing from the past,' I said quietly.

'Well humans don't belong here!' shouted the robot harshly. With that I was thrown into a dark gloomy dungeon.

After a few hours I found a glistening key! I was about to turn the key but heard footsteps...

Ruby Condon
Colindale Primary School, London

Ruby And The Great Escape

I was doing my homework when I fell into my page! *Thump!* A lady ran to me and was baffled by my appearance. I was taken to a palace that proudly shone in the sunlight. Inside sat Queen Victoria with her face screwed up! *The Victorian times,* I thought.

She shouted, 'Lock her in jail, she's a spy!'

I sat in the cell on the grimy bench, wondering when I'd be free. A swarm of flies hovered, I instinctively followed them. My book! Where did that come from? *Whoosh!* The page sucked me back in. Oh no! Where to now?

Nicole Court
Colindale Primary School, London

Robots Are Ruling

During a stormy afternoon, two boys were playing a ball game outside their homes. The thunder clapped and a string of lightning went straight for one of the boys. It was too close, one of the boys got hit. Next stop the *future!* He felt the sting of an electric fence and inside was what looked like a robot guarding a prison. Seemed he liked the future. He was abandoned in a prison cell. A guard fooled the boy and lured him into a room with nothing of use but a whirring, glitching robot carcass.

Aaron Mehta (8)
Colindale Primary School, London

Attack Of The Menacing Monkeys

Somewhere in a deserted island, a confused, scruffy man called Roan was on the hunt for the famous time machine that teleports anywhere as quick as a flash! It was there! All these years of hard work had paid off! He stepped inside, he flipped the dials years and years back to the year 3096AD. The machine hummed to life! He landed in a field of evil monkeys controlled by Doctor Zephanon. But Roan grabbed the controls and made the robot monkeys defeat their own master! In the end Roan had a happy life and threw the machine away!

Henry Moyns (11)
Cracoe & Rylstone CE (VC) Primary School, Skipton

Doctor N51

In 2001, Doctor N51 was working on a robot to take him back to 1901. He'd been working on it for 5¼ months. It was massive. Two years later, a smelly monster queen farted so loudly it woke up her monster eyeballs and they bounced away like tennis balls. It was so smelly the cars stopped working, the police ran away and burglars came from all over the world. Doctor N51 could not stand the smell and wanted to escape. He unplugged the robot's charger. (Don't forget to switch it off.) He switched the robot on and *boom*. Escaped!

Isaac Critchley (7)
Cracoe & Rylstone CE (VC) Primary School, Skipton

Harry And The Time Machine

Once upon a time there was a brilliant skier called Harry. One day he found a time machine on the top of a really, really high ski slope. He climbed in then he drove the time machine 9,000 years forward. When he got out of the time machine it looked really different to what he thought it would look like. It had no snow anywhere but all the people who lived there were very kind. There was a man called Seb. Seb helped Harry get back to where he was skiing. When he returned Harry was caught in an avalanche.

George Butcher (7)
Cracoe & Rylstone CE (VC) Primary School, Skipton

The New Planet Find!

Once there was a girl called Anna and a bird called Sunshine! Anna had powers to travel in time!
One day they both travelled to 5792 AD. When they arrived they saw people heading up to planets! Then they both jumped into a rocket and they set off! After, they spotted a new planet! But their rocket broke. Suddenly, they were on the strange planet. Then a Martian appeared! He helped them fix their rocket, then Anna and Sunshine flew back to 2182 AD in the rocket and became famous! They named the planet Caceal and now they live there!

Emily Butcher (9)
Cracoe & Rylstone CE (VC) Primary School, Skipton

The Magical Shed

'This is boring!' whispered Sebastian gloomily, as the teacher spoke. Time dragged on, at least for him it did then finally it was break time. Sebastian rushed over to his friends. 'What are you doing in here!' He spotted them in their overgrown shed. 'You know you're not allowed in here...' Suddenly they found themselves in a strange-looking place. 'Where are we?'
'I don't know,' said Poppy excitedly.
'But look,' said Emily happily...
Moments later they heard somebody calling, but who? A castle was on fire!
'We have to help!' So they did and saved Victor and Victoria...

Evelyne Roche (9)
Cracoe & Rylstone CE (VC) Primary School, Skipton

One Magical Life!

There once was a family of three and they all moved into the Yorkshire Dales and moved into a castle. When they put their baby to bed a vampire ghost popped up and scared the baby so bad it cried in fright. Super Woman saved the day and teleported over to 2016 and the mother had another baby called Emile. They were now in Hawaii and they had a lovely house at the beach. When they were swimming they got eaten by the magical time-travelling chocolate shark and ended up getting chased by a fluffy dinosaur in his tummy!

Amelia Mackenzie (11)
Cracoe & Rylstone CE (VC) Primary School, Skipton

Princess Poppy And The Monster!

One day Queen Isabella was in the garden by the river. Meanwhile, Prince Charles was sitting on the grass with Princess Poppy.
Later on Charles and Poppy went to the beach. Just then, while Charles and Poppy were having lunch, a terrifying monster rose from the sea. He was ginormous. Just then, he stabbed Poppy very hard and Charles was upset. He went home and Queen Isabella was very upset too. But unbelievably, she forgave him even though she was not expecting it and so Charles and Queen Isabella were very happy for the rest of their lives.

Francis Roche (7)
Cracoe & Rylstone CE (VC) Primary School, Skipton

The Unusual Police Box

One day there were three boys called Toby, Charlie and Will. When they were walking back from school they saw a police box. That police box was unusual so Toby opened the door. They stepped into the police box and it launched into space. When it landed they were in the future. They were struggling a bit because they'd never been there before because it was their future. But they found where they were meant to be going. They were in London's Big Ben, hanging from its clock. They could see the police box. They cut the rope and returned.

Tom Hartley (7)
Cracoe & Rylstone CE (VC) Primary School, Skipton

What Just Happened?

One day George and Scarlet were learning about Victorians in school. George and Scarlet went outside and saw the sun. They ended up in the Victorian times. A person saw them and thought that they were slaves, but they weren't slaves... The man said in a cross voice, 'Get back to the workhouse!'
They tried to explain that they weren't slaves but it was too late. When they went into the workhouse they saw the king. The master said, 'These aren't good.'
Then the king took them and was about to chop their heads off but they disappeared back home!

Isabella Huck (9)
Cracoe & Rylstone CE (VC) Primary School, Skipton

40

The Amazing Dream

Once three boys called Jacob, Jack and Tom, and a dog called Dot, went for a walk in the woods. Jacob spotted a tree that he hadn't seen before. Dot started climbing the tree, Jacob went after her. Jack followed them. All of a sudden, Jacob slipped and fell down to the ground. Tom panicked, he ran to help Jacob but Jacob was crying out in so much pain. Jack quickly climbed back down the tree followed by Dot. Jacob suddenly woke up in his bed. 'It was all a dream!' he said to himself. He drifted back to sleep.

Jack Robson (9)
Cracoe & Rylstone CE (VC) Primary School, Skipton

The Fairy Tale Kingdom

Once upon a time there was a magic world and under that place there was a little girl named Violet. She wanted to be a fairy princess and it came true. She was at a fairytale kingdom. She loved the world until she heard a sound. She took a look and she saw a woodcutter. She shouted across the room, the fairies came straightaway. Then there was a bright light, it was a fairy, a magic fairy. She magicked the woodcutter away. Then the fairies were going home and the girl woke up again.

Lucia Barnes (8)
Cracoe & Rylstone CE (VC) Primary School, Skipton

The Ghost Problem

Once upon a time there was a boy called Zak. He lived on a farm which was a creepy farm because there were spiderwebs everywhere and a basement which had a ghost.

One day Zak's friend disappeared. Everyone was scared and wondering who was next. Another sound came. It was horrible, it said, 'You are going to die!' Everyone was even more scared. They huddled up and suddenly the lights went out and they were that scared they cried out for their mummies. Then they realised the ghost was talking to the gummy bear he was eating.

Zak Martin Mackenzie (7)
Cracoe & Rylstone CE (VC) Primary School, Skipton

Death In The Future

Once there was a man called Jeff. He lived on a farm. There was a storm one night and there was a flash.

The next morning he was feeding the pigs but the pigs weren't there! He saw a flying time machine. He wanted to ride it, so he did. He went to 77777 but the machine shut down. So he found some people but he did not know that they were evil. When he was fixing it the men where about to kill him but the Indians found out and they came but it was too late.

Harry Lancaster (8)
Cracoe & Rylstone CE (VC) Primary School, Skipton

The Papyrus Paper

'Finally!' breathed Georgia, heavily. The girl with golden hair and blue eyes. 'We have got to the riding stables,' puffed Georgia to her grey mare Jasmine. As Georgia entered the arena on Jasmine, she curiously whispered to Jasmine, 'That's weird, nobody's here today.' Suddenly, Jasmine broke into a gallop and then... *Pow!* They found themselves in Ancient Egypt. While they were walking along the sandy streets, they came across a papyrus paper maker and he said that his delivery got mixed up with the cobbler's. So Georgia had to go get more reeds. 'Wow!' said Georgia, 'We had fun!'

Olivia Barnes (11)
Cracoe & Rylstone CE (VC) Primary School, Skipton

Digital World

It was a mysterious, gloomy night.
I went to my mum's dusty old attic where I found a shiny, old-looking contraption. I blew decades of dust off.
The Halloween-like contraption spoke, 'Hi, where do you want to go?' Without thinking, I pulled a spooky lever; off I went. I was in the middle of a time war, life against death. Then I looked closer, it was a digital time war. Blood was everywhere, squelching beneath my feet. People were dying.
'Where am I? Will I die or will I survive? I want my mummy!' I screamed because I was scared.

Ayomide Francis Aleshiloye (8)
Eton Park Junior School, Burton-On-Trent

The End

Astro and Callum were in Callum's dad's garage when a small light appeared from an old broken dusty box. Astro and Callum were very curious. Astro and Callum opened the box. There was a small box in it. It had a red button. Callum pressed it. *Grinding, whirring, bang!* They were in a strange, smelly place. Astro looked up and saw a robot. It came to them – everybody was strange, little, clumsy robots. *How did we get here?* Callum thought. *Will we ever survive?* They panicked and cried. Then they saw the box and hit the button, *bang!*

Kanye Bennett (9)
Eton Park Junior School, Burton-On-Trent

The Short Journey

In the darkest night, I went down to drink some orange juice. Then I didn't feel like sleeping so I went to the attic. It was right at the corner of my eye. It wasn't there yesterday. I gazed at it then I pressed a button and then... *Boom!* I landed on a rocky landing. Then I saw the king of the lizards, the T-rex. I ran as fast as I could. I saw a portal so I jumped in. But I floated to space and I teleported. I was tired so I went to bed and slept peacefully.

Thaiyub Ali (8)
Eton Park Junior School, Burton-On-Trent

The End Of Doom!

I saw it standing in the corner of my attic. It wasn't there yesterday. I blew dust off to reveal a strange contraption. It looked weird. I took the cover off. Instead of handles there were buttons. I pulled the door open. Darkness. Darkness surrounded me. The ground started to shake like an earthquake. Not long after I heard a horrific roar. I got up and saw a dinosaur in my head. I thought, *How will I get home? Will I survive? Will I even get home? How did I even get here? Why, have I even done something bad?*

Liberty Grace Morris (8)
Eton Park Junior School, Burton-On-Trent

The End Of Castles

I was cleaning my room. I finished. I fell asleep. Darkness. I heard a thud on the floor. I quickly woke up in surprise. I was surrounded by grey bricks. There was a pink and blue room. Where was I? *Does anybody live here?* I thought to myself. I was tired, I went to find a bed to go to sleep. I was finished looking around.
'How do I get home? Where am I? How do I get out of here? Will I survive this? Will I ever get home? I whispered quietly.

Lilly Baker (9)
Eton Park Junior School, Burton-On-Trent

The Contraption...

Instantly, I saw something there deep within the basement. It looked odd. It looked strange. It stood there looming over me. I could hear rattling. I went forwards. I saw a lever. It glistened and glowed. I pulled it. The contraption began to shake and wobble. I began to shiver and turn. I walked out. I was no longer in my basement. Darkness. Darkness surrounded me. I could barely see anything. The ground began to shake. *Where am I? How did I get here? What is that? What is this place? How and why is it so dark?*

Ellie Walsh (9)
Eton Park Junior School, Burton-On-Trent

The Time Machine

Suddenly, I saw something in the loft. There was lots of very strange stuff there. It was very creepy. Then I saw a strange machine. Without even thinking I pressed a button on the machine. It made very strange noises, crunching, grinding, then *smash!* I fell with a sickening thud. Darkness surrounded me. I heard lots and lots of roars. I was 100% sure I was not in the loft. My heart pounded rapidly. No longer was I in the loft.
'How on Earth did I get here? Why am I here? Will I survive? When did I get here?'

Kabeer Ahmed (10)
Eton Park Junior School, Burton-On-Trent

Battlefield 3

I woke with a bang. I fell to the floor. The magic thing was in front of me, it said, 'Time Mover'. I'd seen it but it was spooky, it was automatic. It was small, it had one button so I pressed it and *kaboom!* Gone! I saw blood, nothing but guns and blood on the floor but I got up. I was in a battlefield.
'Get up and fight soldier!'
'Where am I? How did I get here?'
'Come on get up, you've got to take cover or you might die. Come on, move, move or you will die!'

Jack Gaunt (9)
Eton Park Junior School, Burton-On-Trent

Dino Age

I found an unknown machine in my shed. It was looming above me. It had all sorts of different levers and buttons which were multicoloured. I touched it and it made a funny sound. I opened it. I fell over and it was a weird experience, it lasted for ages. Whiteness. I was surrounded by darkness. I was on the floor. But all of a sudden I saw dinosaurs and I ran for my life. *Where am I? This isn't my shed. How do I get out? How did I get here? Mum help me. Get me out of here!*

Bradley Ferris (9)
Eton Park Junior School, Burton-On-Trent

The Dinosaur Of Doom

I saw it immediately. There, deep in the attic, stood something; looming beside a pile of books stood a strange cupboard. It wasn't there yesterday. As I inspected, a golden handle glistened. I pulled the sparkling handle. Grinding, crunching then *bang!* I fell to the ground with a sickening thud. Darkness, it surrounded me. The ground shook beneath my feet. My heart pounded rapidly. No longer was I in my attic. *Roarr!* Looming above me was a T-rex. It looked very hungry. I screamed. *How on earth did I get here? When did I get here? Will I survive here?*

Hiba Ahmed (8)
Eton Park Junior School, Burton-On-Trent

The Prehistoric

Woah, this is creepy. It's freezing in the basement and there's a lot of stuff down here. I wonder who had all this stuff. But what's that? I definitely know it wasn't here yesterday. So I inspect it, there are buttons. Without thinking I press one. Then suddenly a crash. *Thud! Thud! What's that noise?* I think to myself. I open the door and what is that? There is a falcon with no hair and bigger, there are more thuds and a bit more and a bit more. Woah, what's that... ? I want to go home.
'Mummy, help me!'

Jake Neal (8)
Eton Park Junior School, Burton-On-Trent

48

The Amazing Time Machine

I saw it in the corner. Something was there. It looked like it.
'Surely it's not!' I said to myself. 'It can't be, can it?' I found it in
Ancient Egypt, it was a weird shape and it was stuck in the sand.
Brightness. Sand covered me. In the distance I saw a man, it looked an
Ancient Egyptian person. He looked like a weird person. How did I get
here? Will I survive? Will I ever get back? How many hours will it take
me to get back home safely? Will I see my lovely parents ever again?

Reece Goodison Legrice (9)
Eton Park Junior School, Burton-On-Trent

The Best

I went further, further down. It was there. I called it 'The Magic
Unknown Machine'. It was so magical. It was so cool. I saw it. I walked
towards the unknown machine. I walked in. I pressed the red button.
I fell on the ground with a thud. I gasped, I stood. I walked forward. I
found a cute candy dog. A mint bird. It was a miracle. My dream came
true, it was the best ever.
'Why am I here? What am I doing here? Well at least it is amazing.'
A big thud. It came towards me. *Bang!*

Courtney Owen (10)
Eton Park Junior School, Burton-On-Trent

Untitled

Kanye woke up with a fright. Something strange appeared in the corner of the room covering the contraptions. Kanye gasped, *What is it?* he thought. Was he dreaming? Without thinking, he ran out of his bedroom.

He was in the middle of a field, guts everywhere around him! Kanye ran into the Viking hut. He got stuck there. He tried to get out from the Viking times. He couldn't get out. Then his mum called him and he came back. It was all a dream. He went downstairs for breakfast and he played with his friends in his back garden.

Callum Ryan-Jones (9)
Eton Park Junior School, Burton-On-Trent

The Time Traveller

I saw it instantly, there in the corner of my room. Looming over my books stood a mysterious square-looking box with a blanket covering it. It wasn't there yesterday. As I inspected it, I saw many buttons instead of door handles. I gasped. *What is it?* I thought. Without thinking, I pressed a button. *Bang!* I fell. Darkness. The ground shook, my heart pounded. This was not my room. Wind screeched. A flying car! *No way!* I thought. *How did I get here? Will I ever get home? Why am I here? Will I survive? I want my mum!*

Zeb Fern (9)
Eton Park Junior School, Burton-On-Trent

Zombie Apocalypse

There I saw it. It was an unknown contraption. It was hiding behind the books. It was on top of a dusty pile. I was curious about the contraption. It had a bloody lever. I pulled it, nothing happened. I pulled it again and then *bang!* It was dark. I could hear something. Zombies! What? I couldn't believe what I could hear. It was ominous. *I can still not believe it,* I thought. I screamed to death, 'How did I get here? Where am I? Am I going to survive?' I was scared. 'Argh! Noo. Help me please!'

Zaki Muhammad (9)
Eton Park Junior School, Burton-On-Trent

The Robot Who Cried Red

Instantly, I woke up finding myself in a mysterious place. It was the desert. Right in front of me sat an unknown robot who always cried red. The machine was a silver-coloured robot. The wind howled. Just then he disappeared immediately. I couldn't see the mysterious robot. I went to the cave but there wasn't any sign. The clue was nowhere to be seen, *Maybe he could be next to the palm tree,* I thought. Just near the cave there was large footprint noises. Out came a caveman, it was massive; it was roaring very, very loudly.

Esha Ahmed (8)
Eton Park Junior School, Burton-On-Trent

The Future

I saw it instantly, it stood in the corner of my dad's room. Looming with buttons, levers and wheels, the mysterious machine called 'Future Machine'. I thought and forced myself to press it. I wondered what it could be. *What is it?* I pressed the button. I gasped loudly. Darkness. It surrounded me. The ground shook beneath my feet. Rapidly, my heart pounded. I was flying in the air. *Where am I? How did I get here? Am I going to get home? Am I going to survive?* I thought. *Am I going to see any person here?*

Skye Lang (8)
Eton Park Junior School, Burton-On-Trent

The Mysterious Machine

I saw something mysterious and dusty in the corner. I had never seen that before. I went closer and closer. There was dust on it. I knew it wasn't there yesterday. I had a long thought. I wanted to touch it but I was scared. I had to touch it. I touched it. It took me back to Victorian times. I had never been there before. An orange monster popped out. I wanted my mum. I screamed, 'Help! Help!' I screamed and yelled but no one came for me.
Then someone came. 'Are you okay?'

Taibah Jaleel (8)
Eton Park Junior School, Burton-On-Trent

The Exploring

I went in my grandpa's spare room. There it was, it was always there and I never knew. A mysterious machine. I didn't tell anyone but I saw two buttons. The left side was orange. The right side was blue. I didn't care, I pressed it. I went inside. Why did I go? I was looking where I was. I saw dinosaurs roaring. I grabbed a girl and said, 'Come.' I got the machine and inserted the key. She had it. I put it in, the monster smacked it away; it went into the deep, deep sea. We were stuck!

Ali Azhar (9)
Eton Park Junior School, Burton-On-Trent

The Girl And Her Dream

She saw something move. Anneesa's dream. She had never seen nightmares. But today she did. It was there. It looked like a strange mask. It took her to Ancient Egypt to find out. It looked exactly like Tutankhamun's mask. What if it was? But she didn't understand anything. People stood there watching her as they carried a strange thing on a plough. She was all confused. An unusual boy popped out of nowhere. He asked her, 'What is your... '
Instantly from the pyramid came Cleopatra. Annesa screamed. What would happen to her? 'I'm scared. I want to go home.'

Sumeya Bibi (10)
Eton Park Junior School, Burton-On-Trent

Dinosaur Land

I saw it in the toilet making spooky noises like a ghost. I kept hearing creepy noises. I opened the door. It was a machine. Without thinking, I opened the door. Inside was a strange machine. I pressed a colourful button. As quick as a flash, it took me somewhere else. I was in the dinosaur land. Dinosaurs surrounded me, guessing who I was. It looked like they were friendly dinosaurs. They were sniffing me. The machine was making noises. A dinosaur grabbed me in its teeth as if it was going to gobble me up, but it didn't…

Musa Muhammad (9)
Eton Park Junior School, Burton-On-Trent

The Discovery

As I walked into a large dusty room of coffins, out of nowhere I saw Tutankhamun creep in. Tutankhamun, the boy king, came towards me. As I stood in horror, someone snatched him! He suffocated to death! Breathtakingly, I saw him rise up. Stumbling towards me and shouting angrily he said, 'Get out now!' But I was trapped!
Just then his wife came and said, 'You dare enter this tomb.' Suddenly, he threw me out! I landed in my room. I said, 'Where was I? Was it a dream?'

Bryn Davies (10)
Eton Park Junior School, Burton-On-Trent

54

The Discovery

Exhausted, I found myself walking through the Valley of the Kings. The Sahara desert, abandoned and scorching-hot. Looking up, I saw the humongous pyramids. I knew I needed to explore the tomb further of boy king Tutankhamun. Creeping silently into the tomb, the fragile twinkling precious ornaments caught my sight. Tutankhamun entered through the wooden door and started to run. All of a suddenk, I was screaming! I just about escaped before boy king Tutankhamun turned me to stone. The Egyptian king found his jewellery and was pleased. He trundled back to his coffin and never came back.

Alex Skinner
Eton Park Junior School, Burton-On-Trent

The Eruption

Bang! I was leaning against an unbreakable cave as an egg rolled past. I followed the egg not knowing what was inside it. Suddenly I realised something terrible was coming! It was the edge of the cliff! The egg started to shake. *Crack-k-k-k!* The egg hatched and out came a purple dinosaur.
'Move it, soldiers.' Villagers from far behind were shouting, 'Seriously, we need to hide!'
I said, 'Quick, I know, I saw a cave somewhere, let's go!' In a flash, the dinosaur shrank!
'Amazing,' I said and we both started running.
'Show yourself!' The king had found us...

Neha Ahmer (9)
Eton Park Junior School, Burton-On-Trent

Viking Land

As I got up I saw pots, glasses and an old kitchen. Suddenly, I lifted my head up and looked around to find that I was in a different place. Before I was at my own house but now I was on the floor in an unknown place. Slowly I got up and started to look around. Wherever I was I wasn't in a normal house. Suddenly, I heard a voice coming. I looked around, terrified. There was nowhere to hide. Trapped! I got it! As I got under the table, the door creaked open...

Aneesa Atiya Khan (9)
Eton Park Junior School, Burton-On-Trent

The Mysterious Space Discovery

One day I opened my eyes and found I was in space. There were planets of all colours, shapes and sizes surrounding me. Mars, Neptune and Venus, all of them were surrounding me. Meanwhile, there were creepy sounds of footsteps that weren't mine and suddenly there was a loud voice.
'What are you doing here?' exclaimed the spaceman.
'I'm just on a discovery Sir,' I said nervously. The creature was looming over me. I could not believe what he did next. He started coming towards me with his mouth wide open. Inside were some glistening sharp teeth...

Suhayla Khalifa (9)
Eton Park Junior School, Burton-On-Trent

The Journey

I ended up in this type of desert, you could say. But then I realised I was in Egypt. I could see a woman in the distance. So I walked further. It looked as if she was homeless, so I decided to help her. I went to the pharaoh and he said she was poor, so he made her homeless. He said he would only give her a home if she would work as a maid for him. I went back and explained to her. She was very happy and she agreed.

Samia Iqbal (10)
Eton Park Junior School, Burton-On-Trent

Ancient Adventure

Bang! My journey ended and my adventure started. I was in my time travel machine. I opened the door and looked around. I couldn't believe I was standing in Ancient Egypt! Suddenly, soldiers grabbed me. Minutes later, I found myself in a cell. It was really small. Guards came and told me I was going to be punished for murder. I knew I didn't do it. Someone walked towards me.
'You may leave!' said the person, 'And never come again.'
'Who are you?' I said,
'I am the Pharaoh Tutankhamun,' he said.
I was shocked!

Hooriah Majeed (10)
Eton Park Junior School, Burton-On-Trent

Space Adventure

It thumped! My heart thumped quickly. I opened my eyes. Suddenly, I saw an area with just holes in the ground as if it was a home of a creature. Me and my crew wondered where we were and how we got there. I remembered I was touching that machine in the attic. I ran quickly around me. Then a rocket appeared next to me. I started to see what was around me. Quickly I ran to the edge, there was Earth! Suddenly, I saw someone, it was an alien! They started running towards me. More started getting close...!

Lilly Fotheringham (9)
Eton Park Junior School, Burton-On-Trent

The Jurassic World

I slowly opened my eyes. Then I discovered that I was back in time. My eyes saw leaves around me. The sun was scorching. My tummy was rumbling and I needed some food. I searched everywhere. Suddenly, I saw a massive egg. It was the same size as an ostrich egg. I crept up to it and grabbed the egg and took it with me. Suddenly, an eye opened. Soon I realised it was a dinosaur. I looked at it with horror. I started to run as fast as I could. All of a sudden a pterodactyl darted at me...

Isiah Muhammad (9)
Eton Park Junior School, Burton-On-Trent

The Jurassic Run

As I woke up, I didn't know where I was. Peering outside, I walked slowly out the cave. I heard a noise. 'Rooooaarrr!' I looked behind, all I could see was land. But then there was a dinosaur. I ran towards the jungle as quick as I could. I stopped.
'Come and get me,' I said to the dinosaur. I kept on running and singing a song to myself. 'Run, run, all I need to do is run.'
The dinosaur caught up. I made a sword out of stone. The dino was close. I stabbed it!

Harvey Greenough (9)
Eton Park Junior School, Burton-On-Trent

The Spaceman

I woke up in a strange place. A man looked at me square in the eye. His name was The Spaceman. After a while, heat spread on my skin, it was the sun! The Spaceman said to get out of the spaceship immediately. Our spaceship blew up and we only had ten minutes of oxygen left!
'Oh I wish Dad was here!'
Just then, The Spaceman told me to close my eyes. When I opened them, I was in my bedroom!
'Oh gosh that was only a dream!'

Shamil Nadeem (10)
Eton Park Junior School, Burton-On-Trent

Egypt Mission

One hot, sunny day two agents were walking and their boss called and said that a mummy was on the run. They couldn't find the mummy so they asked the agency for GPS signals to find him. When they found him, he had a gun and it chased them and said, 'Why are you following me and stopping me from walking?'
They didn't know what he was saying. They injected him and he wouldn't wake up. For their reward they got jets to go anywhere they wanted. They had their own private jets to fly by themselves.

Mustafaa Baig (9)
Eton Park Junior School, Burton-On-Trent

The Wonderful Ancient Egypt

As I woke up, I saw I was in Egypt. I looked around and saw lots of pyramids around me. I felt so excited because I always dreamt of going to Egypt and discovering about Egypt. But then something really bad happened! Some terrifying mummies had come out of nowhere. I ran and ran until the balls of my feet were tired out. When I was out of breath I sat on a big black rock and tried to be friendly with the unattractive mummies.
After a few minutes, the mummies were my friends.

Nisha Ahmed (9)
Eton Park Junior School, Burton-On-Trent

The Curse Of Cleopatra VII

As I stood there in silence, I was wondering where I had ended up? I soon realised that I was in Cleopatra VII's pyramid. I looked around at the hieroglyphics but couldn't understand them. Suddenly, she got up and came out of the bandages into her real form. Her glistening black hair waved. I started to run but she caught me. I asked a question.
'Why are you chasing me?'
'My soul won't rest until I eat you alive!' she answered.
I fainted, thinking it was my imagination. But was it? Was it real?

Imaan Hussain (9)
Eton Park Junior School, Burton-On-Trent

Wild West

On Saturday, I was walking by the local butcher's. A bet was going on. I decided to join. They were betting over this person called Jack Auther. Apparently, he was undefeatable in duels. I thought to myself, *I will not be able to beat him.* So I only bet ten coins. The bet went on! We got ready. Back to back, we took five steps. I shot! But I missed! I took another shot, I missed again! I was done for! I ran as fast as I could into my house! I knew as I entered I was done for...

Amaan Shazad (9)
Eton Park Junior School, Burton-On-Trent

The Mysterious Night!

One day I woke up. Next to me was my companion Maxis. As we rose, we saw that everything had been destroyed. Fire was burning down the houses. As soon as we remembered everything, Maxis tried and tried to open the door but it was no use.

After minutes of trying, we both kicked at the door, it went down. 'Come on,' called Maxis. Inside we saw a huge teleporter with strange symbols. After a while, we managed to get the electricity to the teleporter and tapped the red button. We teleported to our own dimension...

Ikraam Abid (9)
Eton Park Junior School, Burton-On-Trent

The Mysterious House

One day I was in this house. I went in this room and there was Queen Elizabeth. She was going to chop somebody's neck off. Then she saw me. She told her soldiers to come and get me. They got me and put me on the chair. I had almost been chopped up but then this little boy had stopped the Queen. The little boy pulled me off the chair. We ran away. We quickly went home and we would never ever go there again!

Malaika Ali (9)
Eton Park Junior School, Burton-On-Trent

Sneeze-Rex

As I was looking for some chickens and sticks, I walked deeper into the forest. Finally, I found some but as I was strolling back... *Roar!* Suddenly, a dinosaur appeared. Before long, I grabbed the chicken and ran for my life but it was too late. I was already in his mouth! Then I remembered, I had a chicken! I plucked off a feather and tickled the dinosaur's mouth. Quickly, the dinosaur sneezed me out and I was gone, already deep in the forest. When I returned home, I had some delicious chicken for my dinner.

Urte Bagirova (9)
Eton Park Junior School, Burton-On-Trent

The Attack Of The Dinosaur

It was dark, I saw nothing. I'm in my cave with no food. There was no way out of this. All of a sudden I was hungry for food. How could I live? *Roooar!* At that moment, he knocked off my roof. Suddenly, he grabbed me with his tiny hands. Just then, I stabbed him and he went down with a bang! How did I survive? Without going far I could eat lots of food. As time went on I wondered how could I get back? I also met a big cat who was my pet cat.

Cameron Gilbert-Gallagher (9)
Eton Park Junior School, Burton-On-Trent

The Tomb Of Tutankhamun

As I opened my eyes, I found myself in the Valley of the Kings. right in front of me was Tutankhamun's tomb. People say whoever opens the tomb of Tutankhamun shall be cursed. Let me see if that is true. As I opened the tomb, the mummy suddenly came out. It started to chase me. I ran as fast as I could but it caught up with me. I had never seen anything like this in my life. I accidentally stood on the mummy's strap and it turned into dust!

Samir Haider (9)
Eton Park Junior School, Burton-On-Trent

The Magical Time Travel

One day, in a magical land, there lived a gorilla called Drunkling. Drunkling was very strong and smart. One day he fell in love with a gorilla called Lisa, she was a princess. One day Drunkling saw Princess Lisa from afar and he shouted, 'Will you marry me?'
Lisa answered by saying, 'Of course!'
Then suddenly a magical time machine came from out of nowhere and Lisa got sucked into the time machine. Then Drunkling said, 'I will get back my wife today,' and he did so. When he got her back Drunkling was relieved and lived happily ever after.

Tofunmi Majekodunmi (10)
Grangewood Independent School, London

64

Red, Green, Blue And Yellow Buttons And A Lever

One dark and stormy night, lightning struck the house as it grew a face and swallowed an innocent girl walking past. The girl looked around, trying to find an exit. In what she presumed was the stomach she found a machine, it had red, green, blue and yellow buttons and a lever. She pulled the lever and voila! She was somehow transported to the dinosaur age. She lost her ring under a stampede of dinosaurs. She found her ring in a well and the well transported her back home, back to her sweet hometown.

Christabelle Routley (10)
Grangewood Independent School, London

The Stone Of The Future

'There it is, the stone of the future,' said Drake. Drake reached out for the stone and touched it. Automatically he was transported to the future. In the future it was realistic. First of all everybody was wearing high-tech stuff and they were also riding on segways. Drake was the only one who looked odd. He thought how was he going to get back? He looked around then he asked an old man in a jumpsuit for some money and a segway so he could fit in.
After two hours he had the stuff. Next stop... Las Vegas!

Antoiné Charles-Joseph (10)
Grangewood Independent School, London

Mission: Roman Empire

'Hello, commander speaking, do you copy?'
'I hear you loud and clear,' replied Agent Delta.
'Mission accomplished!' Commander Colonel announced proudly, 'All thanks to you, Agent Delta.'
At this point Agent Delta's mine was racing, as he was on the trail to the Agent Hall of Fame! *Whoosh! Flash!*
'Hey guys, where did Agent Delta go?'
'Agent Delta, you have been selected as the greatest spy in the agency!' said a robotic voice.
'Have I?'
'Yes, you will now enter a random era.'
Kabam!
'Remember to keep your formation.'
'Romans, charggge!' shouted a centurion.

Joshua Omokhuale (10)
Grangewood Independent School, London

66

Time Travel

It was a dark and stormy night. I was running away from an angry mob of people just because I borrowed a time travel machine to demonstrate it was fake. To do that, I needed a person – myself. I quickly went to my secret lair. There, I switched on the 'on' button and pointed the machine towards myself. I found myself screaming as I saw a dinosaur. So immediately I sent my body to the future by mistake. I was in the year 3015. So again I pointed the machine at me but... it did not work!

Cristian Alexandru Rarinca (10)
Grangewood Independent School, London

The Strange Monster

One night in an old city there were two girls, Sophie was one of them and Scarlet was the youngest. A few days ago they heard a strange sound, so they went outside. It was pitch-black, so they brought a torch just in case. They went in their garden, Scarlet screamed, she saw a monster. It said, 'What are you doing up now?'
Scarlet ran away, she held onto Sophie so she ran with her. They were home safe, but they were lost for about an hour.

Sienna Hadlow (9)
Halstead Community Primary School, Sevenoaks

Dan And The...

There, a century long, long ago, stood a little boy named Dan. He saw a dark hole and he went over to it and it sucked him up and there, standing in front of him, stood a dead robot. He wanted to get out of this hole but how? *Bang!* He had a brilliant idea. He was going to find some tools to make Bot alive again. He found some tools. But did Bot help him get our? Yes, it did. Dan went to tell his family.

Georgie Keeble (10)
Halstead Community Primary School, Sevenoaks

Nikki And Her Time Friend!

One day Anne Boleyn arrived at Nikki's high school because Anne had tripped herself and fell into a time machine. Nikki didn't know Anne was there until she lost her diary and bumped into her while looking for it. Anne had found Nikki's diary and started writing in it. This made Nikki suspicious about Anne having it. When Anne returned to her time, the postman knocked a box over and Nikki's diary fell out and she saw it near a flowerpot. She was so glad she found it! Nikki promised herself she would never lose it again...

Hannah Wiggins (10)
Halstead Community Primary School, Sevenoaks

The Tudor Times

Once there was Henry VIII and Jane Seymour, they were married to each other. The other day Queen Elizabeth got into an argument with Jane Seymour because Jane Seymour wanted to be queen. Queen Elizabeth said that she could be queen because she had been queen for years. King Henry came and stopped the argument and that was good. What he did was he sat them down and chatted with them one by one, and they were fine. He said, 'Stop arguing with each other!' They all became friends again.

Brooke Callow (9)
Halstead Community Primary School, Sevenoaks

The Terrible Tudors

One terrible day, I was walking along an old, stinky street. All of a sudden, a smell of pies hit my nose: it was King Henry with his gleaming, gold jewellery. I was shaking; my heart was pounding as fast as possible.
'Send her to prison *now!*' Henry demanded. Unfortunately, I was stuck in prison and I couldn't get out. But suddenly I could hear a voice in the corridor.
'Sir Henry has sent me to chop her head off!'
It was scary. Then completely out of nowhere, I squeezed out of the bars, never, ever to be seen again!

Millie Elizabeth Digby (10)
Halstead Community Primary School, Sevenoaks

My Space Journey

Suddenly, I am on the moon! Where is this piece of advanced technology? Where could it be? *Boooom!* What was that? Oh no! It's a gargantuan rocky asteroid! Quickly, I need to find that piece of technology. It's getting closer. Where is it? No. I'm going to die! What's that? It's the piece of technology. A laser beam. I can use it to destroy the asteroid. *Zaaap!* The asteroid is gone! Now let's get back to Earth. When I get back I am rewarded with a whopping £1,000. And that is my best space journey of my life.

Teddy Poole (10)
Halstead Community Primary School, Sevenoaks

The Ancient Roman Time In The Stadium

There's a little boy called Jeff who wanted to be the best gladiator in the world. So he went in the stadium and beat the third best gladiator in the world. So he put a thumb down and a death machine came out... it was a lion!
Was the lion good enough to beat Jeff? He lived his dream, will it stop now? No! He is unstoppable. Nothing can stop him. The lion charged. Jeff picked up a shield and a sword and charged at the lion, and stabbed it and it died. He was a champion!

Harrison Jones (9)
Halstead Community Primary School, Sevenoaks

Futuristic Failures

Once, in the future, a very incredible robot was made. Its controls were very hard but it was harmless; apart from the explosives armed in him. His name was... Jimmy!

Later on, Jimmy heard a rustling sound and it triggered his defence system... poor rabbit!

About five minutes later, Jimmy was tearing the city down! What would everyone do to stop him? A few minutes later, Jimmy tore down a building and a piece hit his 'shut off' button. Nobody knew what to do except a toy who turned Jimmy back on with a paper aeroplane, causing no damage anymore!

James Samuel Storkey (10)
Halstead Community Primary School, Sevenoaks

The Troublesome T-Rex

There were two cave people, Chloe and Alex.

One day they went to pick berries, only to find a T-rex! They ran back to their cave just in time because the T-rex found them! All they had to eat was a few berries. Soon, the T-rex started to moan. It turned out the dinosaur was lonely and just wanted to be friends! So the children came out and made friends. They had to come up with a name... it was Rexster because he wrecked a lot of stuff! He was so grateful that he decided to guard their home forever!

Megan Wakeling (10)
Halstead Community Primary School, Sevenoaks

The Two Cities

One day there were two cities, one underneath the other. That day someone from down low went up top to explore; when something went wrong. Someone asked where he was from and the person from down low told him, but then he had to show him. That night the person from down low showed him and now he had to stay there. But he really wanted to see his family again.
The next night he snuck back up but got grabbed. Who was it? Was it someone from up top or down low...?

Antonie Goldup (9)
Halstead Community Primary School, Sevenoaks

The Return Of Sjib

'OK! Preparing for landing.' *Crash!* 'This is T Tenny reporting... anyone?' *Thump!* Suddenly T Tenny found himself on a strange, green planet. He scanned the area and noticed a white house of some kind. He ran to the house and smacked on the door, even though it didn't look like one. There was a quiet beep, then the door blew up and four ki blasted flew out! T Tenny jumped to the side, a strong figure named Sjib flung out and threw a ki blast at him. He bounced in the air and ki blasted him; he appeared behind him.

George Herbert (9)
Halstead Community Primary School, Sevenoaks

72

Into The Unknown

Hunting, the last hope. Mindful of a curiosity. Surrounded by vegetation. A booming noise rippled across the ground – he wasn't alone... Shadows formed into a roaring beast. Trailing behind the caveman, shadows followed. Heart racing, face streaming with sweat, he scarpered into his own comfort. Brimming with fear, his cave had an unsettling feeling. Concern eased by the sweet sound of silence. Yet was he alone? Another shadow passed the cave, what was it? Footsteps patted the ground. Louder and louder, they didn't stop. A screech of noise echoed through the cave. He was no longer alone...

Aliya Forde (11)
Halstead Community Primary School, Sevenoaks

Mysterious Charm

The Khalifa charm. I've heard of it but never seen it until today. It was found by some bright spark in an old forbidden tower. Legend has it only the gold-hearted descendent can achieve its true powers to travel to places you desire. Problem is there's no gold-hearted descendents found, until today. I was able to touch the charm and the most extraordinary thing happened, my heart desired a place warm like the beach and buildings made of jewels, and before I knew it I was there. You guessed it, I was the only descendent left to rule.

Hussain Ahmed Ali Khalifa (10)
Hospital Education Service, Coventry

The Royals

There was no warning! We were under attack! We were all ushered into the safety room underground. Prince Lawrence flicked the light switch. Suddenly, there was a *thud!* The whole room filled with terror. My mother, the queen, called out to me, 'Are you OK Princess Olivia?' Prince Lawrence turned the switch on. Eventually, we plucked up the courage to step out! We realised when we stepped out, we looked at the Eiffel Tower! By magic, we'd time travelled! We were in Paris! My family and I stared at people dressed in Victorian attire. We had travelled back in time!

Priya Pal (9)
Hospital Education Service, Coventry

The Doctor

It was a very hot day. I saw the Doctor's TARDIS. I jumped into his TARDIS very quickly, when I saw the Doctor. He took me to his home, Galifray. When I got there I saw Daleks. 'Let the battle begin!' said the Doctor. Sonic screwdrivers boomed, Daleks crashed and we defeated the Daleks. Me and the Doctor were so happy, but unfortunately he had to take me home to Essex. When we got there he gave me a present. I opened it steadily. I was so excited. It was my very own sonic, blue, colourful, blasting, cool screwdriver.

Rhianna Grew (10)
Laindon Park Primary School, Basildon

The Magic Wall

It was Christmas Eve, I was leaning against the wall. I was in the past. There I saw Jesus. I was there before the angel came so Mary thought I was the Angel Gabriel.

I went back home. I looked at the story about the past. I'd changed the story so I went to the past. Gabriel the angel helped me change the story back. But then I couldn't find the door so I asked the angel to help again. I went back and checked the story. Everything was back to normal. That was a good adventure I'd had.

Ella Kelsey Shanaj (10)
Laindon Park Primary School, Basildon

Effortless Egypt

I woke up to see a statue. I opened it up, it was a time machine. I quickly jumped inside but sneakily a crazy scientist came in with me. I set the dials back to 3100 BC when Ancient Egypt started. I jumped out but quickly realised I'd messed up. I had landed on Tutankhamun, killing him at eighteen years old. Luckily, the scientist realised the machine was broken so he fixed it. When we went back in time I saw pictures that changed my whole life. I was now called the Pharaoh Killer.

Sonny Daly (10)
Laindon Park Primary School, Basildon

The Key

'Hollie, there's a key in the hamster's cage!'
'OMG, let's try it in your wardrobe.'
We opened the wardrobe and there was an icy castle and ice guards.
'Attack!' called the guards. As we grabbed the torch, they all moved
back and opened the tall icy doors. A tall figure stood in our way.
'You will never escape alive,' said the figure.
As we chased it around it started melting. 'Noooo!' it said.
Then we ran home and locked the door, chucked the key for the next
victim to find and to not take seriously. You're next!

Lillian Vankassel (10)
Laindon Park Primary School, Basildon

The Last Match

Thud! As Leonardo hit the floor of Planet Football, he stood up to see
his team waiting for him but in the corner of his eye, he saw the alien
team training. He went over to his team, they told him they had been
challenged to a game of football and if they lose, Earth gets blown up.
Every shot Leonardo's team had it didn't go in the goal, same to the
alien team but in the final two minutes, Leonardo got a smashing pass
from his team and scored. The match ended and the team from Earth
won again.

Freddie O'Connor (10)
Laindon Park Primary School, Basildon

Into The Future

Whiz! Bang! Poof! There I was, face first in the future. I had somehow teleported there and couldn't get back. I stepped outside and saw cars, not even on the floor. I looked around for my lab and I saw a man. His hair was everywhere and his face was a dead ringer of mine. I went over and he pulled out a time machine and said, 'I've got a time machine and I'm not afraid to use it!'
I told him what happened and he let me have it. When I got home, I realised I'd just met myself!

Alfred Kneller (11)
Laindon Park Primary School, Basildon

Only A Small Time Left

Opening the time travel door, I find myself back in Anglo-Saxon times. I want to have fun but I can't because time's running out. Oh no, my feet are stuck. I pull until finally my feet unstick. Jumping into the time machine, I begin to start the engine, staring at the time left. Only three minutes left until I vanish forever. The engine finally starts to move. I am shaking with fear as the time goes down really fast. Landing on the ground, knowing time is moving, I jump out and change the time limit to 'unlimited' for future use.

Keira Edwards (10)
Laindon Park Primary School, Basildon

Tudor Trouble

I found a time machine next to a bin. I pressed a button and when I opened my eyes I saw a castle. Without moving, I was grabbed by my arm. I blacked out. Next thing I knew I was in a cell. Luckily, there was a broken bar. I squeezed through and ran. I was chased by a fat Henry VIII and a bunch of guards. I pressed the button on my machine and I opened my eyes. When I looked down, the machine was gone.
The next day I could see a book which said, 'Prisoner Alex's escape.'

Alex Mintram-Chattell (11)
Laindon Park Primary School, Basildon

Guilt

Thud! I looked up, I knew I shouldn't have hopped on Mum's time machine but I couldn't stop myself. To my left I saw a gleaming blue iceberg! I was on the Titanic! The captain offered me a room. I spent the next night thinking whether or not to tell them about the iceberg. I decided to tell them. The captain was so shocked he fainted. When he got back up, he steered the ship to safety. Nobody died that night and I have lived with the guilt ever since, living in an alternative reality!

Joel Singh (10)
Laindon Park Primary School, Basildon

Going To The Future

Ding, dong! It was the clock! Me and Danielle ran to the clock hidden in the attic.

'Time to go to the future!' explained Danielle. We jumped into the clock and went to the future!

'Hey look! A flying car!' I cheered. We jumped into it and off we went. But the car wouldn't stop! We flew around like mad! 'Oh no! There's a wall!' we screamed. The car crashed right into the wall. The car fell to the ground. Luckily, we weren't hurt! To our relief there was the clock! We jumped into the clock! We were back home!

Caitlin Springer Porter (10)
Laindon Park Primary School, Basildon

The Future Killer

Thud! I slammed against the floor. Had I travelled to the future? I looked at the rough wall of bricks, there was a wanted poster. A killer was on the loose! There was a black figure in the foggy distance. I followed it down the alleyway. Dead bodies were everywhere, it was the killer! I looked around to find a knife. I stabbed it. Suddenly a girl, who looked like me, walked out of the distance. I followed her. We came to her home where I saw the time machine. I pulled the lever to disconnect it from my family.

Charlotte Coomber (11)
Laindon Park Primary School, Basildon

A Slight Change Of History

Walk! *Slip! Smack! Shabang!* And there I was standing in the harsh trenches of World War II. I looked up. I saw planes firing. I looked backwards and saw a Nazi running at me with a rifle. He had the gun at my head but then he slipped, shot his rifle in the air at a plane. It fell into a tank, the tank shot the teleporter out the nozzle and onto my head. *Whizz! Shabang!* I was back in 2015. I went to Raj's shop and thought it was a dream, I grabbed the paper, I'd won the war...!

Bobby Anderson (11)
Laindon Park Primary School, Basildon

Where's Santa?

Huff, puff, pant! I looked around. Were they gone? Santa's Elves? Boy were they vicious in the 13th century! I breathed in the bitter cold Arctic wind – exhausted. Suddenly, a spindly hand grabbed my elbow.
'Where do you think you're going?' cackled an Elf evilly.
I struggled to get out of his reach but failed. He dragged me to a hole under the ice.
'Where's Santa?' I shouted.
'Who's Santa?' said the Elf confused and slammed the ice cap shut.
I'd gone back too far in time it seemed. Santa didn't exist yet! How was I to get back?

Ira Saxena
North Primary School, Colchester

The Magic Racket

It was Charlie's thirteenth birthday. Grandad gave Charlie a tennis racket. Why? He was not good at sport. Grandad said it was magic. Charlie was sent to tennis camp. They played matches every day. He won every match he played. He couldn't believe it. They entered him into Wimbledon. He won all of his matches and got to the final. In the final he lost the first set but then he went on to win the match. He was so excited. After the match Grandad said, 'Congratulations! By the way, that was never a magic racket!' Then he went home.

Charlie Cassar (10)
Oratory Preparatory School, Reading

Sinking Beneath The Rolling Waves

The warmth surrounded me; cool air conditioning ran through my hair. The corridors twisted around the endless facilities. The boat rolled slowly. Mama had sent me to get the menu from the dining saloon. I pushed open the door onto the deck, and was greeted with a huge volume of water. It smashed over the railings, and flooded down the stairs. Screams, shouts, cries echoed around me. People rushing to the lifeboats, fighting against the wardens. Suddenly, the boat shuddered, it started to tilt upwards. I screamed, 'Mama!' But it was too late, the last lifeboat smashed against the iceberg.

Charlotte Amelia Harrison-Moore (11)
Oratory Preparatory School, Reading

The Revival

Crash! Hades and his Underworld followers came again to kill Zeus. They wanted his power. In all the other attacks Zeus had remained firm, but not this time. He fell. Perseus knew what he had to do if he wanted to revive his father. He would have to go down to Hell to get a pink powder and put it on his father's face. The journey was long and treacherous and he had to pass through many dangerous places. He had a fierce battle with Hades, but came out on top and obtained the powder. His proud father ruled again.

Angus Parke (11)
Oratory Preparatory School, Reading

The Bombing

John sat in the house listening to the screams and shouts outside. He trembled in fear. Suddenly, a huge explosion sounded around him and the house collapsed. Chunks of brick fell down. He screamed before darkness consumed him. He didn't know how long he'd been there, maybe hours or even days! The thought terrified him. Then suddenly a small shaft of light poked through. A face appeared through the gap. They stared at each other. Then John asked, 'Is the bombing over?' The man replied, 'Yes boy, not only that, the Germans have surrendered. The war is over, you're safe!'

Dominic Robert Martin (11)
Oratory Preparatory School, Reading

Pop Star's Disaster

Once there was a pop star called Lizi. She had a Chihuahua.
One day she was getting ready for a concert. She got changed and put on make-up and then she was ready. She went on stage; thousands of people were watching. She started to sing. It went well at first but then her Chihuahua, Fifi, escaped from her dressing room and ran on stage and knocked over the microphone, pulled down the curtain and ran off! Everyone thought this was part of the show and cheered loudly. After that, Fifi came onto the stage for every performance.

Isabella Powell (10)
Oratory Preparatory School, Reading

The Trial

'Do you plead innocent?' asked an officer.
'Yes Sir, I do,' I replied.
The officer wrote something down in his notebook. 'What is your reason for deserting?' he asked.
'I didn't desert them, I had a mind blank. I wasn't thinking,' I argued back.
The officer wasn't satisfied. 'A trained soldier should be able to control his emotions!'
I was expecting this. 'Sir, may I mention that since 1916 we didn't get trained. We got trained to use a rifle, then sent over here.' This shut the officer up. I knew I was lucky. Many others hadn't survived this trial.

Fraser McAdden
Oratory Preparatory School, Reading

Vera Lynn

It was 1941 in the darkest days of the war. Jimmy and I walked towards the Black Lion. We were both in army uniform. We ordered egg and chips with a pint. Vera Lynn was there and a crowd gathered. She strummed her guitar and started singing, 'We'll Meet Again'.
Suddenly, we heard the air raid sirens ringing in our ears.
'Quickly, get to the shelters!'
We ran to the back of the pub and tumbled down the stairs into the bomb shelters. I'd never again get the opportunity to hear the singer who was known as 'The Forces' Sweetheart'.

Keira Cater (11)
Oratory Preparatory School, Reading

Attack On London

Grandpa's machine was absolutely amazing! It was yellow in colour, with a lever. I blew off the generations of dust that clung to the machine and read the 'Do Not Pull' sign over the lever, but of course I pulled it. Suddenly, I was blown off my feet. I slowly got up but I couldn't feel the tarmac floor. Tarmac? I was in London, a billion years in the future. I was a robot. Just as I had become used to this sensation, a voice called out, 'Help, help! They're upon us!' It was then that the metal foot descended...

Will Tibbs (11)
Oratory Preparatory School, Reading

84

Great Grandad And Me

I saw something small sticking out of the old, dusty book of my great grandad's that I hadn't seen before. Gasping, I read the haunting poetry...

Let others have the tale to tell, of sands so red from shot and shell...

The words swam in my head. Blinking twice, I looked up to see the ocean swell, crashing left, and swirling right. The captain yelled, 'Bombs away!'

Looking at his face, I instantly recognised those determined blue eyes. 'Oh my goodness! It's my great grandad!' Turning left I saw horror... how had I landed on this foreign, bloodshed beach?

Amelie Limbert (10)
St Joseph's Catholic Academy, Pontefract

The Final Goal

It's here. Tiredness dances gracefully like fairies in the players' determined minds. Lining up unremarkably in the classic 4-4-2 formation, England are raring to go for extra time. Gottfried Dienst, the referee, sets extra time running. 96,462 pairs of eyes are here. Passing it around dominantly, England are playing well while West Germany struggle impatiently. The extra time whistle goes. The spectators talk restlessly about the exciting game. Finally the second half starts. Geoff Hurst, who is going for his hat-trick, sprints down field and... *Goal!* The famous line rings vociferously, *They think it's all over! It is now!*

Eli Saul (11)
St Joseph's Catholic Academy, Pontefract

Time That Was Lost

'Wow! A time machine!' Ash gurgled gleefully as he stepped into the lagoon of mystery. Ash set the time to 'Robin Hood' and off he went. Ash arrived in the dungeons of Sherwood and smashed a gate that he thought was the gate to outside, ready for thrilling adventures.
'Oh?' pondered Ash as he saw Robin Hood gleaming at him.
'Hazar!' Robin Hood chimed as he walked through the gate. 'Come on, let's go to my crew!'
When he had met everyone, Ash waved goodbye and headed to the time machine. When he got home he went to sleep!

Isabelle Fay Duguid Devlin (11)
St Joseph's Catholic Academy, Pontefract

Untitled

I sit enjoying the ice cream out of the tub. Just to defy my mum as she never lets me eat out of the tub; she insists that we use bowls. It tastes so much better out of the tub, the flavour seems much better along with the texture. All along I am wondering when Mum will be back and spoil my pleasure? The front door opens – is it Mum? I jump up and look. No, it's Dad – back to enjoying the ice cream. The dog, Flash, begins to bark. Yes! Where's that bowl? Quick!

George Walsh (11)
St Joseph's Catholic Academy, Pontefract

The Bizarre Fire Of London

In a small cottage in London in 1666, Mary and Martha were complaining that none of their jumpers got sold.

Later that night, Martha smelt something burning. She raced upstairs and woke Mary. Afterwards, they rushed downstairs to a large fire. They didn't know what to do until... 'I have an idea,' yelled Martha, 'get that jumper! You can use it as a fire blanket!' And so she did and because it was so thick it worked. Imagine if that really did happen at the Great Fire of London! That would be very bizarre!

Faith Harrison (10)
St Joseph's Catholic Academy, Pontefract

Where Am I

'Doctor, Doctor!' echoed Eric, excitedly running and giving himself a great sweat on his face.

'What if the dinosaurs weren't slammed by an asteroid in the Cretaceous period?'

'Well you see Eric, we wouldn't develop our brains because we would be dominated and eaten due to lots of dinosaurs. Secondly, dinosaurs might be able to learn things like football, so they'd probably be smarter or even bigger.'

'I want to see it.'

'You want to see it? I'll send you on your own.'

'Wait, noo...'

Dr Richard was relieved and Eric vanished like a ball swiftly.

'Wait, where am I?'

Ziane R Vailoces (10)
St Joseph's Catholic Academy, Pontefract

Into The New World!

There's something misshapen and overgrown inside me. I only allow it to come out in the dark when I'm alone. I worry about the ramifications of my presence here; Halloween is upon us and it's my time to go – into the future that is. I walk through an enchanted portal that takes me to the radiant future. As I walk through, all the noises stop abruptly. I'm nearly there! My feet step onto a bare floorboard and a cold shiver runs down my spine. A room full of old, rusty pots is where my haunted body frame stands, still.

Tilly Lumb (10)
St Joseph's Catholic Academy, Pontefract

The Christmas Truce

Britain and Germany were at war but on Christmas Eve in 1914, they stopped fighting and dropped their weapons. They sang Christmas carols like, 'Silent Night' and there was even a burial service for dead English and German soldiers. Both sides even gave gifts to each other, mostly food. On Christmas day, a football match was played between both troops. It was begun by a British soldier who kicked a football out of the trench; then the Germans joined in. Unfortunately, at midnight, a flare was lit to tell the soldiers to return to fighting and the war carried on.

Emily Whittles (11)
St Joseph's Catholic Academy, Pontefract

Number 37's Adventure

One day an alien named Number 37 woke up to be startled, as during the night he teleported in his new bed to an orphanage! As he studied his surroundings, he saw that a hole had sprouted; numerous storms had occurred. Thankfully, he had plenty of time to rack his brains and come up with a plan... As night approached, Number 37 only just came up with a plan; bizarre though it was! Unfortunately, he was forced to sleep in the loft, a shockingly gruesome wreck of a place. When everyone was asleep, he clambered on the roof and jumped!

Rubén Walters (10)
St Joseph's Catholic Academy, Pontefract

A World War II Surprise

I woke up and I felt that something was not right. I didn't have any clue so I went to my wardrobe where I saw a shiny red button inside, which I was eager to press, so I did... I disappeared in a spark, then found myself on a bench and I wondered where I was.
'1939!'
That's when I fainted.
After an hour, I woke up and a general came up to me saying, 'This is the Second World War, here you go.' He gave me a helmet.

Mason Yarsley (10)
St Joseph's Catholic Academy, Pontefract

To War

One day Isabel and Molly were having a sleepover. They were bored, so they went outside and saw a gap in the bush. They went through a light and they were in World War I! They saw Joey, the horse from 'War Horse'. They looked around.

'We're in War Horse!' shouted Isabel, 'But we've gotta get out before we get killed!'

Looking around to see if there was someone to help them get out, they saw that everyone was shooting at each other.

'Let's go through that wire,' Molly pointed to some wire and they went through and were home!

Isobel Sykes (10)
St Joseph's Catholic Academy, Pontefract

Charley's War

'Charley, focus all fire on that trench.'

'OK Joe,' Charley said nervously, wondering if the rest of the men could tell he was scared?

'This tank isn't going to last any more hits from that LMG,' said Len, worryingly.

'Mortar!' said Joe knowing they would be some of his last words.

Boom!

Charley leapt out of the tank at the last second, narrowly escaping the blast. Len and Joe were dead! He laid on the floor but he knew he needed to get back to the trench. He got up and sprinted back. He was safe but for how long...?

Charles Ingle (10)
St Joseph's Catholic Academy, Pontefract

A Mistake In Time

2010. On a typical morning an ordinary man pushed open a door, only to find that he had been teleported one millennium into the future! The environment around him suddenly changed, it looked like a futuristic nightmare house. As soon as he got out of the labyrinthine house he saw skyscrapers that towered into space, cars that could hover and surprisingly go underground, but the thing that captured his attention was hardly any form of life, mostly robots.

Hours went by but he could see no one, so he just had to live his life there, lonely and miserable.

Edwin Andrew Knight (10)
St Joseph's Catholic Academy, Pontefract

Dinosaur Danger

One day my friend and I climbed to the top of my house! It was phenomenal until my friend fell and grabbed immediately onto my new, expensive coat sleeve.

'Argh!' we screamed until suddenly we fell on a dinosaur's back. We wondered what to do, when suddenly the dinosaur flung my friend so high she flew home rapidly. I tried various things to get home: swimming home, getting the dinosaur to fling me home, flying on the dinosaur's back home and jumping home. None of these worked. I had to wait years on end, eating dead bodies...

Molly Mackenzie (10)
St Joseph's Catholic Academy, Pontefract

Charlie's War

'Keep firing Jim!' screamed Charlie. Jim and Charlie were battling the Germans at the Somme in their trustworthy tank. The tank was under heavy fire from a German Gatlin gun shredding through the armoured apparatus as it forced its way through No-Man's-Land.
'It's gonna blow!' shouted Jim, 'Jump!'
The two men leaped for their lives out of the small hatch at the top of the mechanism, onto the war-torn piles of bodies and mud.
'Jim... Jim... Jim?' screeched Charlie, only to find his friend bleeding out on the disease-ridden earth.

Matthew Smalley (10)
St Joseph's Catholic Academy, Pontefract

No Way Back!

I woke up this morning with the startling feeling of needing the toilet. So I went. As soon as I touched it, I shrank down to a quarter of my size. I fell in, to find it was a time machine. I passed out to find myself in some sort of future. The cars hovered, planes were spaceships, that could travel at the speed of light. Buildings could float and tower above the sky... I was getting frustrated because... how could I get back?

Ethan Caine (10) & Reuben
St Joseph's Catholic Academy, Pontefract

Back To History

Night and day, soldiers were fighting until today. One soldier went out of his trench; he was carrying a football that his son had given him to remember him. A German soldier came out of an opposite trench, they began to set up the goals.

After a while, they started to play; nobody was still sat in the trench, everyone was taking part. Guns were peacefully placed in the trenches, no piercing cries of death and one ball kicked everywhere. Ecstatic noises were made and the wind was rapidly moving like in a race. War has ended, World Cup began!

Mateusz Broszko (11)
St Joseph's Catholic Academy, Pontefract

The Mystery Time Machine

After tea, I sprinted down to the basement where I saw a machine covered in lots of stuff. I cleaned the dirty things that were covering the machine – I noticed it was a time machine; I went inside to take a closer look, when suddenly I got trapped inside it! I couldn't escape but when I tried to think, I unexpectedly knocked myself out and landed on a button.

When I woke up I wasn't in the basement, I was totally in a different place, which was really mysterious. Where was I? How would I get back?

Radley Yabut (11)
St Joseph's Catholic Academy, Pontefract

The Peculiar Tunnel

Tom and William were having a mundane day, when suddenly Tom saw a very peculiar tunnel. It was dark and mysterious. When they reached the tunnel, Tom climbed in and called William to join him. They walked through until they faced a blank wall so had to go back.

Suddenly, William fell down a hole and Tom went after him. When they landed, they were in 1942. It was night-time, German bomber planes were overhead. Because they were in a street, a woman heard them and took them indoors.

How could they get home...? Would they return home...?

Nathan Winwood (10)
St Joseph's Catholic Academy, Pontefract

Devouring Dinosaur

James was trapped in the time machine. A monstrous dinosaur suddenly approached it. The dinosaur sank its fangs into the half-broken underwater time machine. Water leaked in rapidly. Now James could see the spear-like fangs of the colossal killer. The dinosaur banged its head into the glass and nearly shattered it. Immediately, an enormous school of sharks all bit the dinosaur and dragged it away. Blood drained out of the beast. James gasped. The water had already got to his waist. James sprang out and crashed through the ice, and landed spread-eagled. The ice started to crack...

Oliver Pang (8)
St Nicholas Preparatory School, London

The Match

In this stadium, Santiago Bernabeu, I'm watching the dirtiest match ever. There are fights continually. There have already been 19 yellow cards and 6 red cards, it is not even half-time yet. First of all it started at the sixth minute with two players grabbing each other by the neck and it even started a fight in the crowd. Some people even have to be evacuated, such as the king and queen, so they do not get hurt in the fight. Thankfully, I am the other side of the fight but I see every second of it. I like it.

Marius Tezier (10)
St Nicholas Preparatory School, London

Back With The Dinosaurs

When I came back from school, I ran to my room and I found a beautiful gem right on my desk. I touched it, and I vanished into another world. I walked around and saw dinosaurs walking around. A dinosaur was behind me with massive jaws, tiny hands and a scaly tail. It made a large growl. I picked up my speed and saw some blue mist. I turned inside and appeared in another place. A shadow appeared with bloody jaws and muddy claws. I thought I was safe but I wasn't. A growl. Wish me good luck!...

Laura Lopes
St Nicholas Preparatory School, London

Race Car Aliens

One clear, dark night a curious girl was looking through her telescope at Saturn. She looked through her telescope day after day but on the 5th day she realised Saturn's rings aren't just ice and rocks but they were actually race car tracks for aliens!

A week later the information was out and everyone was flying in their outstanding car with food and drinks when they wanted! The girl, who found out the information about Saturn's rings, also invented flying cars. The people and aliens agreed that every Sunday they race. Soon the girl became the master of amazing space!

Zoe Weiler (9)
St Nicholas Preparatory School, London

The End Of The Dinosaurs

Doing my daily duties, going to trees to munch up leaves. Suddenly, I see it. A shower of red fire balls. I roar and run but I'm thrown in to darkness. I wake, but the world I stand on is of complete ashes. No trees. No water, no colour, only rocks. Soon the survivors will turn to the graves that my friends, family and enemies turned to.

Oscar Tracey (9)
St Nicholas Preparatory School, London

Egyptian Adventure

'Psshh!' Bob entered the time machine. Today's adventure was travelling. He arrived in front of the great pyramid. He entered silently. Inside were mummies everywhere! Bob saw a few guards. Luckily, they didn't attack him at first. But... 'Attack!' roared the pharaoh. Bob ran as fast as a cheetah. But the guards were catching up... *They're going to get me*, thought Bob. Bob started to get really scared. He was pretty sure that they were going to catch him and make him one of them. But Bob managed to reach the time machine but stupidly forgot to close it...

Abel Bijaoui (9)
St Nicholas Preparatory School, London

How Is Life In 3015?

In London 1917, Jaydon 003 was from MI6.
One day an enemy stole the MI6 time machine. He threw Jaydon in it. For five hours the time machine flew through space. Finally, Jaydon heard the machine announce, 'You are now in 3015!' Jaydon came out of the machine and was really freaked out! Jaydon was surprised to see Robo Man. Jaydon met the Robo Man. They all frowned at him, they all whispered. Then they attacked him! Jaydon went all around Piccadilly Circus but he still never found his or the MI6's time machine. He was lost forever, on Mars...

Emma-Rose Albertini
St Nicholas Preparatory School, London

Trapped By Vikings

A normal day, Lucy, a young girl from London, was in bed sleeping. She heard a noise and opened her eyes, Lucy saw a group of Vikings looking at her. She thought they could have trapped her. Lucy gulped and looked at her arms and legs. She was tied up with rope! Lucy tried to move and she managed to stand up. The Vikings left Lucy alone; Lucy made ten jumps towards a room on the boat and found a time machine. She jumped in it and managed to push the 2015 button...

Gloria Scarioni (8)
St Nicholas Preparatory School, London

Dr Fizzy's Adventure

One night Billy Fizzy was not tired. He crept silently out of bed. He wanted to go on an adventure. He ran to his time machine! Billy went back in time to a creepy forest. Suddenly, a crocodile bit his leg and wouldn't let go! Billy had magic powers and floated up to a tree. Then a monkey slapped his face! Billy instantly became... Doctor Fizzy! He leapt over a swamp and swung on a vine. *Whoosh!* Billy was instantly in his room again and now he was super tired. He lay down in his soft, comfy bed and snored.

Alissa C Lopes
St Nicholas Preparatory School, London

The Time Computer

Dan played with his computer. Today was a special day: he was about to get a new Minecraft server. Dan pressed 'play'. A flash leapt out of nowhere. Dan saw nothing...

He awoke and found himself inside a 'Blocky World'. Dan wondered, he was in Minecraft! Suddenly, an unrecognisable creature announced, 'You will have to get the crystal in the cave of Endermen to get back through the time machine.' He knew where that was. What was this time machine? At the cave, Endermen were everywhere. Dan dodged so he wouldn't provoke them. He saw it...

Alexandra Maugein-Yu (9)
St Nicholas Preparatory School, London

War In The Past!

I was in Leningrad in 1941, walking around the park. It was a sunny day. I travelled here with my time machine. I heard loud shouting and orders. The German soldiers arrived to start the war. Scared, I hid in the park behind the bench. I didn't know what to do! Suddenly, I had an idea, 'I will go back to my time, 2015, and prepare my soldiers to come back here and fight.'

When I had prepared my soldiers, we travelled back to 1941. My soldiers fought in the war and we won! So we had a party.

Anna-Mariia Lapina (8)
St Nicholas Preparatory School, London

Will David Be Dead?

I stepped into the darkness, into the time tunnel, taking me to 2016. What was going to happen next in the UK now we have a new prime minister? Suddenly, I heard a loud gunshot. I opened my eyes. There, with blood seeping through his shirt, lay the prime minister, dead! Who did this? Why did they do this? I was so scared.
I ran down into the time tunnel. I had to tell the prime minister before he got killed. I arrived and told one of the guards. I hoped he would tell David Cameron. Would he be saved?

Louise Prieuret (8)
St Nicholas Preparatory School, London

Time Machine

In 2007, a boy called Martin wanted to be a detective.
One day he saw something – what was it? It was a time machine. He called Emile and Clemens. They went to get the time machine.
'A time machine!' exclaimed Clemens. They travelled in time. They arrived in Egypt.
'Argh!' gasped Emile, 'We are in the pyramids of Egypt.'
Indeed they were. There were 200 pyramids. They checked in 100 of them.
After hours of looking, they saw an enormous pyramid. They found it! Then they travelled home.
Years later, Martin became a brilliant detective who solved crimes!

Martin Rodriguez (8)
St Nicholas Preparatory School, London

Time Travel

A robot time traveller is discovered by Lee and Rob. What will it do?
I'll go and check it out, thought Lee. So he jumped inside with Rob and travelled to the future... but the bolt of lightning ended his journey to the future.
'Argh! Robots are chasing us!' panted Lee, running past the royal palace, under the table, through the cave and into the lake. Rob ran as fast as lightning, back in time into their house and in bed.
'Phew! That was close, they almost caught us!' Lee said.
'Yes.'

Clemens Chao (8)
St Nicholas Preparatory School, London

The Past Is Not So Great

It was a ghost town. Nobody was there. All of a sudden, there was a loud wailing sound. I quickly took cover. Everyone seemed scared. I tried not to be scared however I didn't know what was going on. Suddenly, there was a big bang; people huddled in the centre of the room. I heard planes. I heard bullets fly rapidly across the sky. Planes fell from thousands of feet high. My heart was in my throat. All of a sudden, the terrifying sounds vanished. Once again there was a wailing sound. People left; I did too. Was it over?

Katie Emily Vincer (11)
Shirland Primary School, Alfreton

The Best Invention Of All

Excitement ran through Mary as she proudly stepped out of her machine. Outside, she noticed the thick, pungent smoke that filled the desolate countryside. After wondering about what to do, Mary decided to find somewhere that looked like the history of Shirland. Eventually she found it, her own house and her own daughter. Delighted, Mary strolled casually through the metal door. Luckily, there in front of her was a machine almost exactly like her own time machine; Lisa had followed in her footsteps. Darkness fell. Kindly, Lisa (Mary's daughter) gave her amazing machine to travel home in.

Evelyn Trow (10)
Shirland Primary School, Alfreton

Into The Future

My brain told me to touch the war artefact. There was a piercing screech from the sky. I saw a huge bomb drop from the sky. A vast sign said, *Happy New Year 3000 AD*. I heard a woman scream, 'It's World War III!' I ran to a big house; I was safe. As I looked down, I saw the artefact still in my hand! I couldn't get it off my hand. It was stuck! I ran out of the building and everything was the same as when all of the bombs had dropped. I was stuck in the future!

Harry William Jacques (10)
Shirland Primary School, Alfreton

Back To The Past In A Mysterious Cave!

Three girls were looking for the Christmas decorations. Molly came across a red button as shiny as Rudolph's nose. Olivia dared her to push it. 1... 2... 3... She pushed it. Where were they? They'd landed in a dark cave where green, fluffy mould dropped from the corners. They walked closer towards the exit of the cave. There stood a strange animal. Then they ran down to the bottom of the cave to collect sticks for the fire. Olivia and Molly stood there; they noticed something red shining – it was the button to take them home.
'Finally, I'm home!'

Sasha Leonie Parker (10)
Shirland Primary School, Alfreton

Ancient Egyptian Journey

Where was I? What had I done? Suddenly, the door slammed open. I was scared. It felt like my heart skipped a beat... Walking through the dark woods, I tripped on a lever. As I slowly pulled it, a light appeared. All I could see was sand. I soon regretted what I had done. Soon after, a whole army of mummy-looking creatures came into a dark cave. I was in Ancient Egypt. A man came with some tools. He tried to mummify me! Another man came up to me and locked me in a tomb. The door slammed open...

Luke Singleton (10)
Shirland Primary School, Alfreton

103

The Story Of Ayrton Senna

These last few weeks I have been making a time machine to take me back to Ayrton Senna's death. Suddenly, a deafening noise filled my ears. *Rumble! Crash! Boom!* I was back in 1994. It was very loud and the sky was blue, unlike Britain which was normally grey. After starting the race, I did lots of overtaking. After a while, I made it to the final lap. There were yellow flags all around, then a red one. I thought, *This is Ayrton. Yes.* I was right, he had crashed and he had sadly passed away.

Nathan Kinnear (10)
Shirland Primary School, Alfreton

WWII Time Travelling

Rapidly, I ran away from my mum in London! We were near Big Ben. I felt myself disappear. I had been taken to the middle of the World War II. I started to walk around the deserted streets of London. What was that noise? I felt a bag over my head... All I could see was the darkness of the black bag. After that, I remembered a man asking for my name. I didn't remember telling him and because I didn't tell him, he hit me hard over my soft, fragile head!

Darcy Wright (11)
Shirland Primary School, Alfreton

Rock 'n' Roll

Where was I? Why was everything different? *Knock! Knock! Knock!*
Who was that? I opened the door and right before me stood Elvis
Presley! I followed the Elvis mob down to where Elvis lived. The finger
struck 12.00.
'This is the last song ladies and gentlemen.'
'Not so fast!' It was Michael Jackson! 'I challenge you to a singing
battle.'
Then wow! It was Stevie Wonder (the blind singer) who could play all
musical instruments.
'Whoa Man, let's all calm down and be best friends!'
Suddenly I woke up, it was all a dream!

Keira Alvey (11)
Shirland Primary School, Alfreton

The Monster In The Cave

I heard the daunting monster outside! In the cave I have been trying to
amuse myself but I'm jaded. I have been confined in here for hours.
I have been trapped in here for two days without sleep. I have been
playing on my smashed iPod which never seems to have enough
charge. All of a sudden, a monster bounded onto me. I picked up my
iPod. I couldn't feel the monster on me anymore. I looked at myself,
the monster wasn't there. The monster was standing on one side of me,
then the other. It was beautiful...

Scarlett Rowland (10)
Shirland Primary School, Alfreton

Year 4000

I woke up in a field of grass. I remembered about the box that had sent me to this year. I looked forward, and noticed hoverboards closing in on me. They started getting closer and closer. Then I heard a scream from a mile away. I noticed lasers flying towards them. In a split second, the hoverboards exploded. Then I noticed a shape coming towards me. What was it? It had a gun in its hand. The bullet was about to come out of the gun. I was about to die! Then I said, 'Will I live another day?'

Finlay Brotherway-Hill (11)
Shirland Primary School, Alfreton

The World Of The Dinosaurs

I was on my way into the gloomy loft, remembering that my dad had told me not to press the red button. I was feeling for the light switch, not really concentrating as I was thinking about my favourite books: Harry Potter, when I found a button and pressed it. I was in the time of the dinosaurs but velociraptors were chasing me. I ran…
Just after, a herd of triceratops trampled them down! I was safe. I saw a red button… I pressed it. I was back in the loft, safe and sound. All I needed was the decorations!

Isobella Ann Hunter (10)
Shirland Primary School, Alfreton

The Famous Footballer

Suddenly Wembley erupted, we were in the final. I ran onto the pitch and went to Bobby Charlton. Was I dreaming? I wanted to see it but the tickets were fifty pounds. I'd put some money to it so then I might be able to go. All of a sudden my dad said, 'Do you want to go?'
'Yes! I really want to go!'
'But only if you pay for your ticket!'
We were going to the ferry after the game. Hopefully we would get there in time. I was so excited. But then I saw...

Adam Bush (10)
Shirland Primary School, Alfreton

The Caveman

The ground shook. I opened my eyes; I didn't know where I was. I started to shake. 'What was that noise?' I was scared. I had mucky clothes and ripped trousers. That noise, I recognised it. I really did. 'I'm sure it's a dinosaur, I know it is,' I said to myself.
Rooooaarrr! That was definitely a dinosaur so I cried for help. I heard voices. A boy found me and seconds after the dinosaur came in the cave, I ran out of the cave, I ran under dinosaur legs. My heart was pounding. I fainted with fear.

Frankie Flockhart (10)
Shirland Primary School, Alfreton

The Past But In The Future!

Suddenly I fell to the ground, my legs felt numb. I opened my eyes and what I saw was a huge billboard with a picture of Elvis Presley. After a while of roaming around the city, I found Elvis Presley. But when I went to speak to him he just said, 'Meet me at noon at Nooby Lane.'
So at noon I went to Nooby Lane and found Elvis Presley. I went up to speak to him about his lifetime experiences. After giving me some advice, he told me a story but suddenly everything went black. I awoke!

Oliver Pilkington (9)
Shirland Primary School, Alfreton

Lewis The Inventor

Grrrr! Grrrr! Lewis' pooch couldn't make it. But Brainy Lewis could, he sprang through the portal. Later, he landed in the Ice Age. High icy mountains covered the stunning plains that had once been green grass. *Roar!* Now a different horror scream. Lewis scampered, sweat drowned him and Lewis couldn't believe it. Lewis had been running so fast he was sweating in the Arctic! He observed dinosaurs clashing mammoths. *Bang!* Everywhere browny meteors struck. Lewis knew that must have been the end! He shut his eyes and hoped. Soon after there was no reply.

Harley Whyman (10)
Shirland Primary School, Alfreton

Time Travelling To The Future

When I woke up, the floor was shaking. I was shivering. Then I found a portal. It spun me round and round until it made me dizzy. I woke up on a sandy floor. I wondered where I was. It seemed like I was in a desert. 'Roooaaar,'

What was that? I ran and ran until I found a cave. I ran in it, it was like my bedroom when my bright light is switched off. There were drips running down my pale face. I was shivering like never before. Then I fainted.

Lewis Rice Taylor (10)
Shirland Primary School, Alfreton

A Surprise From 1945

Bang! Scream! Pop! I woke up suddenly. Where was I? As the last bombs ever recounted in World War II exploded, a looming figure towered over me. Who was it? Without warning, I heard the clatter of clamorous footsteps running towards me!

'A girl? Well I never!' yelled a booming voice. I sat up and was greeted with an unusual surprise; crowds of people surrounding me! I looked around. In amongst all those hundreds of people, I saw me, as a baby, being cradled in my mother's arms. The laughing died down and I seemed to be transported back home!

Elodie Stephens (9)
Southborough CE Primary School, Tunbridge Wells

Sailing With The Vikings

A test on Vikings isn't a great way to kick off the afternoon, Lisa thought, dully flicking her pages. She paused and read out question number ten: 'Where is the place Vikings
go after... ?' She stopped reading and felt very dizzy all of a sudden. She seemed to be falling. *Clunk!* She dared not breathe. The floor felt uncomfortable and did not seem to be...
A harsh, cold voice called out in a Scandinavian accent, 'Put your backs into it, men.'
Where was this place? It was definitely not school!

Sophie Barden (9)
Southborough CE Primary School, Tunbridge Wells

The Treacherous Trip To The Blow!

I was on holiday with my family in Pompeii looking at a dog who was killed. Feeling sorry, I stroked it on the head. *Flash!* The town of Pompeii? The earth was shaking beneath my feet. Could Vesuvius be erupting? The dog was alive, but my family wasn't. A man walked up to me and asked for my name. I told him, 'Isabelle.'
'Run!' he shouted. I put my hand on the dog as the ash came closer and prayed that I would be taken back to my family. Time hadn't changed! I'll remember that forever! Poor Pompeii.

Tilly Ward (10)
The John Bamford Primary School, Rugeley

Chaos And Friendship

I was on holiday in the great city of Pompeii. I saw beautiful paintings. I felt sorry for this girl who died. I went over and held her hand.
'I'm sorry! Whoa!'
Before I knew it, she was alive and I was in Pompeii in the past!
'Thank you. I'm Gracius.'
But wait, I was going to die if I don't get back. Gracius warned me about it. She agreed to help. *Boom!* It's happening now! I held her hand and I went with a necklace Gracius gave me! It will give us friendship. But where is she now?

Holly Williams (11)
The John Bamford Primary School, Rugeley

Lake Of Pompeii's Ash

I was on holiday in Pompeii, and saw a dead man! I felt so sorry and I touched it! *Flash!* I was in Pompeii and met the man, Bobius. Then, I warned him of the danger that was arriving, as he baked a cake. Suddenly, a cloud of ash arrived and engulfed the town! Bobius said, 'What's going on here?' I grabbed him and made a run for it, but the exit was blocked. I thought, *I'm eating that cake.* As I took a bite, both of us were transported back to the future, with the cake!

Brodie Derry (11)
The John Bamford Primary School, Rugeley

The Next Time Master!

There I was, in Pompeii on my holiday. It didn't take long to notice a lovely little puppy frozen. I wanted to keep it, that's how cute it was. The thing is, it made me scared that I would be like that one day. Then I decided to stroke it, which was a big mistake. A ray of light blinded me! The dog came alive. I was astounded! It decided to give me a sudden bark. A grumbling noise deafened me. After I charged outside, an eruption was happening. Then I grabbed the dog and went back alive.

Kieran Hardie (10)
The John Bamford Primary School, Rugeley

Pompeii (Not As You Know It)

Today I went on holiday to the ancient town of Pompeii. We looked around and saw some of the people. I saw a man and I felt sorry for him so I gave him a hug. Next I saw a flash! The man said he was praying to stay alive. He told me to run for my life. I ran towards the golden door hoping it was my way back. It was a massive doorway and I knew it would get me back. When I ran past, it triggered something and there was a flash. I was back!

Demi Elizabeth Wilson (10)
The John Bamford Primary School, Rugeley

The Dog That I Touched

As I was on holiday in Pompeii, I was looking at the dog curled up in plaster. I stroked the dog but suddenly it moved and I was in the old Pompeii. Everyone was laughing, talking. It was a bit sad because I knew what was going to happen. How was I going to get back? This was a problem. I could warn them. So I warned them but nothing happened. I walked down the streets and saw the bubbling volcano. I found the dog. I stroked it and I was back with my family and I was happy.

Jimmy Cartwright (10)
The John Bamford Primary School, Rugeley

End Of Time

I gazed up at Abbius and Emmi.
'One little tap won't hurt. Argh!' *Where am I?* I wondered. I turned around to see two young ladies.
'You look lost darling, can we help you?' said Abbius in a Latin accent. Emmi smiled kindly. I took one look at their clothes, I knew where I was... Pompeii! I had to warn them about Vesuvius. Gently, I told them. I took them to the town square.
'It will explode... now!' Nothing happened. I slept at their house that night. That's when Vesuvius erupted. That's when my life ended...

Harriet Jessica Fellowes (10)
The John Bamford Primary School, Rugeley

113

I Don't Know What To Say

Bang! I have just landed in Pompeii. I don't know what to say. Lava is spluttering everywhere and rocks too! Immediately I run for my life, not realising lava is creeping into the time machine. I start to run towards the harbour. I click a button on my bolt and a vortex from the water appears. Then I jump in, spinning around. On my travel back to the future I see all the past leading up to home.

Ronnie Bevan-Phillips (11)
The John Bamford Primary School, Rugeley

Pompeii Pop!

I am with my friends. We go *boom!* We go to Pompeii. There are lots of people running around, panicking. The huge volcano above the city is erupting. It is throwing out pieces of ash, rocks and fireballs. Terrified, we quickly run for our lives. A nearby workman tells us to get inside and we take cover in the amphitheatre. Will we survive? Will Vesuvius devour us?

Nicola Adams (10)
The John Bamford Primary School, Rugeley

Back To The Past

Boom! Crash! Went my time machine. I got out in a mysterious place. I asked people where I was but they were too busy panicking. I looked around. I was speechless because there were dead bodies on the floor. When I saw the volcano, I saw why everybody was panicking, because Mount Vesuvius was erupting. The lava was spewing out the volcano as fast as lightning. Buildings were being destroyed by the rocks. The dead bodies were covered in ash, so were the buildings. Some people made it out of town.

Caitlin McGahan (10)
The John Bamford Primary School, Rugeley

Pompeii Eruption

Boom! Crash! My time machine crash-landed. James Bond and I flew out like fireworks. We landed in a strange city. We were lost! There were people screaming and shouting. 007 and I were shouting at each other. Suddenly, rocks were falling and ash was raining down on us. Oh no! The volcano was erupting even more! It was like thunder and lightning. 007 and I were screaming at everyone to evacuate. 007 and I were going to die!

Rian Mistry (11)
The John Bamford Primary School, Rugeley

The Past Is Just Around The Corner

'Argh!' I heard a colossal cry come from the people beneath me. I had entered Pompeii in 79 AD. My fully functional time machine had made an entrance! My mission was to warn the people of Pompeii about Vesuvius erupting! At first they didn't believe me; they soon did! Suddenly, the floor started to tremble; the man-eating machine sent out a huge rumble! The monster was hungry and Pompeii and I were going to be his dinner! Tiles started to fall off the buildings! The ash cloud closed in on me! I was going to die...

William Moseley (10)
The John Bamford Primary School, Rugeley

Back To Pompeii

I was on holiday visiting Pompeii. It was a wonderful day to be there. I decided to touch the grey ash person and everything just changed. The guy said, 'What are you doing?'
I'd gone back in time. I asked what his name was. He didn't reply.
I said, 'We need to go.' We ran as fast as we could, the ash was going too slow. After miles of running, we got to the boat. We sailed away. I went back to the future. I wonder what he is doing now?

Reece Hawkins (10)
The John Bamford Primary School, Rugeley

Watch Out For The Mummy

Tutankhamun became pharaoh at the age of nine but he died at the age of nineteen. There are many stories on how he died. He was said to be buried in a tomb. Howard Carter found Tutankhamun's tomb hidden in the Valley of the Kings. When he went to look at the jewels he heard a grunt, he turned around and saw a mummy and ran as fast as he could. Then he hid behind a gold statue. The mummy mysteriously returned to his tomb and disappeared from sight. Was it a dream or was it real?

Niall McHale (8)
The John Bamford Primary School, Rugeley

The Story Of Tutankhamun

A long time ago there lived a little pharaoh and his name was Tutankhmun. When he was nine years old he became pharaoh and he died at nineteen years old. Also he had an advisor called Ay and he had a wife called Annar. When he was nineteen, he was down at the River Nile but he had an enemy, his name was Haremheb. One day Haremheb had a deal with Ay to kill Tutankhamun that might lead to his death. When Howard Carter X-rayed Tutankhamun, he had a damaged head, missing ribs and a bent spine too!

Sam Townsend (8)
The John Bamford Primary School, Rugeley

The Story Of Tutankhamun

Once there was a boy called Tutankhamun. He became a king when he was only nine years old but he was only king for ten years because he died when he was nineteen. There were two suspects: Horemheb and Ay. Howard Carter found Tutankhamun's tomb in 1927. They X-rayed the body and found out he had a bent spine, damaged skull and missing ribs. Ay was Tutankhamun's adviser so he could get really close to Tutankhamun and they think Ay killed him. After Tutankhamun died, Horemheb became king of Egypt.

Harry Ryan (8)
The John Bamford Primary School, Rugeley

The Country

Once upon a time, on a hot day in Egypt, news spread around that a boy had the throne and had become the new pharaoh. Everyone didn't think it was true! A nine-year-old boy leading the country, it wouldn't work! He was called Tutankhamun; his dad, Akehnaton, had left the county in a really bad state. How was a boy going to change the country back to how it was?
Years went past and he did just that. He fixed the temples and bought the old religion back. Yet he died at the young age of nineteen.

Kian Wharton (8)
The John Bamford Primary School, Rugeley

The Future

In Ancient Egypt there lived a pharaoh called Tutankhamun. One day, whilst his servants were busy, he went for a walk to see how other people lived. He found Doc's time machine! He got in and made it go as fast as it could until he ended up in the future: 14th November 2015! Cally was around so Tutankhamun had tea with us and told us lots of interesting facts, things about him and Egypt. After tea, he returned to Ancient Egypt in Doc's time car and we wondered if it was all a dream! But he was in Egypt.

Ava Clark (7)
The John Bamford Primary School, Rugeley

The Dilemma With The Tomb Raiders

Many years ago, in Ancient Egypt, pharaohs stood outside guarding the pyramid.
One day some tomb raiders came floating up the River Nile. They were going to steal the jewellery from Tutankhamun's tomb.
Meanwhile, some pharaohs were visiting the tomb to pay their respects. They spotted the tomb raiders and put them in the king's prison. And for a long time Tutankhamun's tomb was safely guarded.

Alfie Glanville (8)
The John Bamford Primary School, Rugeley

The Story Of Tutankhamun

One day news went around that an eight-year-old was taking the throne from his father and was becoming the 11th pharaoh. He had a lot of work ahead of him as his dad, Akhenaton, had left Egypt in a bad state. Tutankhamun first started on the temples that had once been destroyed. Then, as the years went on, he built his own tomb in the Valley of the Kings and also built a statue. Even though he had a very short reign, he did well because he died at nineteen.

Reece Wharton (8)
The John Bamford Primary School, Rugeley

My Mini Saga About Ancient Egypt

Long ago, in the land of the pharaohs, there was a boy called Tutankhamun. When he was nine years old he became king. The problem was that the new king had some enemies! His worst enemy was Horemheb. He wanted to kill Tutankhamun. So he told Tutankhamun's advisor, Ay, to do the deathly deed. Ay put poison in Tutankhamun's drink and this led to his death. Horrible Horemheb became king.

Alfie Huxtable (7)
The John Bamford Primary School, Rugeley

The Stolen Treasure

There once was a pharaoh called Tutankhamun, he lived with his beautiful wife in Egypt in a huge pyramid along the River Nile. The young pharaoh was very rich and powerful, everyone was jealous. One night, while the pharaoh and his wife were sleeping, they heard a loud noise. The sound was a mummy escaping his tomb to steal all the pharaoh's jewels. Then, all of a sudden, a sphinx came to life and chased the mummy and turned him into dust when he caught him. The Sphinx then gave the pharaoh all his jewels back.

Evie Gretton (7)
The John Bamford Primary School, Rugeley

Egyptian Story

When I went on holiday to Egypt I saw the River Nile and it had pyramids all around it. The River Nile was flowing gracefully. I saw Howard Carter searching for Tutankhamun's tomb and five minutes later he found steps to Tutankhamun's chamber.
When Howard Carter found Tutankhamun's tomb, he realised that it was Tutankhamun, the famous pharaoh. In the chamber there were jewels, gold furniture and a sphinx. They were very beautiful.

Ena Davies (8)
The John Bamford Primary School, Rugeley

Untitled

Tutankhamun was only nine years old when he became pharaoh. Horemheb was jealous because he wanted to become King and to rule all of Egypt. He made a plan with Ay to kill Tutankhmun. A pharaoh witnessed the killing of Tutankhamun. They had to run away from the pharaoh. Horemheb and Ay spent some time hiding behind the pyramids and they even tried to cross the River Nile.

William Lewitt (7)
The John Bamford Primary School, Rugeley

Untitled

Tutankhamun was watching his builders build his pyramid for him. Tutankhamun had his jewels in a big treasure chest. The next day Ay, Tutankhamun's advisor, decided to chuck Tutankhamun's jewels in the River Nile.
Ten minutes later, Tutankhamun had just realised that his jewels had vanished. Tutankhamun had to go on a mission to find his jewels. He found the jewels and danced Egyptian style. He returned with the jewels and everyone lived happily ever after.

Chloe Sparkes (7)
The John Bamford Primary School, Rugeley

Tutankhamun's Birthday

Once upon a time there was a boy called Tutankhamun. He lived in a pyramid in Egypt. Tutankhamun had two best friends called Horemheb and Ay. Today was Tutankhamun's birthday party down by the River Nile. All three of them had a swimming race. Tutankhamun's heavy jewellery pulled him underwater. His two best friends swam back to rescue him and pulled him out of the water. As it was Tutankhamun's ninth birthday, they crowned him Pharaoh and made him rich.

Alex Williams (7)
The John Bamford Primary School, Rugeley

Amy's Letter

I received your letter, Amy. I trust you to let you know a secret. Horemheb and I have made a plan to poison your husband, Tutankhamun. Then Horemheb and I will be Pharaoh in turn. Keep quiet and you may marry one of my sons. There won't be time to finish your husband's pyramid but he will still have a good tomb. We will carry on living by the River Nile, despite the crocodiles and flies. We will get more furniture with our jewels. We could hide our spears in the base of the sphinx if we need to.

Alisha Rose Shepherd-Reddell (7)
The John Bamford Primary School, Rugeley

123

Untitled

King Tutankhamun was a pharaoh who lived in Egypt by the pyramids. One day, when King Tutankhamun went to the pyramid to check on his jewels, he was followed by Ay. He was going to take King Tutankhamun's jewels. Tutankhamun went inside the pyramid and Ay followed him. So Tutankhamun hid inside a tomb and told the sphinx to go and get his soldiers. Ay was caught and arrested.

Aden Mullin (7)
The John Bamford Primary School, Rugeley

Pompeii's Horrible Event!

Look at this burnt-out dog, I bet it's been there for over 60,000 years, I feel so sorry for it, I just want to give it a stroke. *Whoosh!* We must be in the Roman times, I think this is 79 AD. 'Woof!'
'Hello little doggy, what's your name?'
'Stump!'
'What a lovely name. I've learned this is the time when that big volcano exploded and everyone died. How about me and you getting away from here, what do you say?'
'Woof!'
'Come on then Stump, let's go to the water, that's where we will find the boats. Let's go!'

Thomas Hill (11)
The John Bamford Primary School, Rugeley

Time Travel

There was a man called James and he had a time travel device, he used it to go to the time of the dinosaurs. A Tyrannosaurus saw him and he ran. A triceratops saw him and he ran faster. A mosasaurus saw him and he ran even faster. He used his time-travelling device to go back to the future.

Hayden Heyes (7)
The Viking School, Skegness

Stone Age Trouble

One day Ugha Bugha and Saga Maga were hunting and caught a sabre-toothed cat in a net. Suddenly, the sabre-toothed cat broke out and trapped Ugha Bugha and Saga Maga in his cave. The sabre-toothed cat was going to eat Ugha Bugha and Saga Maga. Saga Maga found a sharp rock and chopped the rope the sabre-toothed cat trapped them in. Ugha Bugha and Saga Maga raced back to their straw house. Ugha Bugha and Saga Maga were safe back home in their straw house. At home they ate nice juicy berries and drank water from the fresh, flowing stream.

Maddison Johnston (7)
The Viking School, Skegness

The Storm At The Beach

One day Mr and Mrs James were planning to go to the beach. Benny did not know the secret plan. 'Goodnight,' said Benny and Benny went to sleep.
'Benny?' shouted Mrs James in a cheerful voice and they set off to the beach. At the beach Benny did not feel very well. 'I do not want to build a sandcastle or play in the sea,' said Benny.
'Oh no!' said Mr James, 'I have an idea! Why don't you have a drink?'
'Yes please,' said Benny.
Just that minute, a storm started.
'Oh no!' said Mr James.

Roni May Basker (8)
The Viking School, Skegness

The Dinosaur Age

There is a boy named Marti. Marti has a secret. The secret is he has a portal and he travels to the dinosaur age. Marti sees a velociratpor and shoots it, and runs and finds a hole. He digs to make it a home. Another velociraptor comes and he has blue on him. He names it Blue. Marti sees a lab and it is a very old lab, and Marti makes a dinosaur called the stego-rex. The stego-rex eats everything. Marti then makes a T-rex and T-rex saves dinosaur age.

James Cornelius (7)
The Viking School, Skegness

How To Get Back

'Mum,' said Sam, 'can we go to the event now?'
They set off to the event from the new home. In the car Sam and Mum
saw floating cars. It was like they were in the future.
'What is this?' said Sam, putting on a sad face.
Mum said sadly, 'The new home now is old, we're in the future!'
'How are we going to get back, Mum?' asked Sam.
'I don't know,' said Mum.
A girl came over. 'Hello, I know how you can get back!'
'How do we get back?' said Mum
'In my floating car!'

Pippa Prime (8)
The Viking School, Skegness

25

Years of YoungWriters

YOUNG WRITERS
INFORMATION

We hope you have enjoyed reading this book – and that you will continue to in the coming years.

If you're a young writer who enjoys reading and creative writing, or the parent of an enthusiastic poet or story writer, do visit our website www.youngwriters.co.uk. Here you will find free competitions, workshops and games, as well as recommended reads, a poetry glossary and our blog.

If you would like to order further copies of this book, or any of our other titles give us a call or visit **www.youngwriters.co.uk**.

Young Writers
Remus House
Coltsfoot Drive
Peterborough
PE2 9BF

(01733) 890066
info@youngwriters.co.uk